Bites
Scary Stories
to Sink Your Teeth Into

Bites

Scary Stories
to Sink Your Teeth Into

Edited by Lois Metzger

Scholastic Inc.
New York   Toronto   London   Auckland
Sydney   Mexico City   New Delhi   Hong Kong

ISBN: 978-0-545-15890-9

12 11 10 9 8 7 6 5 4   10 11 12 13 14/0

Printed in the U.S.A.
First printing, November 2009

CONTENTS

FOREWORD
by Lois Metzger   ix

PERPETUAL PEST
by Neal Shusterman and Terry Black   1

GHOST DOG
by Ellen Wittlinger   13

GOING OLD SCHOOL IN THE AGE
     OF OBAMA
by Christopher Paul Curtis   26

ANASAZI BREAKDOWN   38
by Douglas Rees

THE COFFIN DELIVERIES   52
by Kevin Emerson

WHERE WOLVES NEVER WANDER
by Joshua Gee   68

I, BLOODER
by Peter Lerangis   82

ABOUT THE AUTHORS   105

ACKNOWLEDGMENTS   115

Bites

Scary Stories
to Sink Your Teeth Into

FOREWORD

When it comes to vampires and werewolves, what you don't know can bite you.

It is widely believed that vampires are dead people brought back to life. Their sole purpose is to suck the blood of the living, which can turn the living people into vampires, too.

Not necessarily.

An eighth-grade vampire gets his blood from the blood bank in Christopher Paul Curtis's story, "Going Old School in the Age of Obama." This kid wouldn't be caught dead biting anyone —or would he?

Rule #1: It's not enough to watch your back. Watch your neck, too.

Some vampires have their hearts in the right places, so to speak. But others are untrustworthy. How can you tell the difference? It's tricky, as one of them learns the hard way in Peter Lerangis's tale, "I, Blooder."

Rule #2: There isn't always honor among vampires.

If you think a vampire lives in your neighborhood, resist the temptation to pay him a visit. This is something a couple of kids can't help doing in Kevin Emerson's story, "The Coffin Deliveries."

Rule #3: Do not become the "guests of honor" at a vampire dinner.

Werewolves are known to be people who—temporarily or permanently, voluntarily or involuntarily—are capable of turning into wolves. But there's a special kind of wolf that must keep to the shadows and away from the light. The characters in Joshua Gee's story, "Where Wolves Never Wander," find out why firsthand—or first*paw*, as the case may be.

Rule #4: Stay out of direct sunlight. At the very least, use sunblock.

If you find yourself in the company of a werewolf, get away as fast as you can. Do not stop to take a picture on your cell phone. JUST RUN.

Sometimes it may be too late to flee, as two brothers find out in a graveyard in "Perpetual Pest," by Neal Shusterman and Terry Black.

Rule #5: Never remove the silver bullets from a dead werewolf's body.

There are other creatures that can bite, too, such as spiritually possessed coyotes, who are always watching, always alert. This is why you should never take something that doesn't belong to you. When the girl in Douglas Rees's story, "Anasazi Breakdown," picks up an ancient piece of broken Native American pottery, she thinks it's okay to do so.

It isn't.

Rule #6: Don't steal—especially rare artifacts.

Dogs are man's—and woman's—best friend. Maybe you have a dog. Maybe you have more than one. But it's important to own a *living* dog. Ghost dogs are not nearly as friendly, especially when they're upset about something, like the dog in Ellen Wittlinger's "Ghost Dog."

Rule #7: You can't teach a ghost dog new tricks.

"Once bitten, twice shy" is an old expression. But you don't want to get bitten even once. There are seven stories about bites in this book. As you'll see, sometimes one bite is all it takes.

—Lois Metzger

PERPETUAL PEST

by Neal Shusterman and Terry Black

"Don't be stupid," Rudy said. "Dead people can't hurt you."

Mark nodded nervously. Sure, in the clear light of day, that made logical sense, but now, with the moon casting shadows over the rusty wrought-iron gates of Perpetual Rest cemetery . . . well, the whole thing seemed nuts.

"Maybe we should go home," Mark said, backing away.

Rudy just laughed and scrambled up the fence, climbing hand over hand, then vaulted to the other side. He landed on his feet like a cat and said, "Hand me the shovel."

Mark reluctantly slid the shovel through the fence bars into his older brother's eager grasp. Rudy, who was four years older than Mark, was a senior at Piedmont High, when he wasn't in juvie, and had the bad habit of doing things without worrying about their consequences. Mark had to admit it was fun sometimes, but other times—like *now*—it reminded him why his brother spent so much time in a juvenile facility, wearing orange overalls behind locked gates.

"This won't really be stealing," Rudy had said, "because you can't steal from the dead, right? It's a legal fact."

There was one reason, and one reason only, that Mark was willing to sneak into the local cemetery and dig up rich people, looking for valuables. He wanted a pair of Sport-Kwest Trainers, the best athletic shoes on the market.

Endorsed by the NBA, worn by the best players, Sport-Kwest Trainers could make any kid a star. *With Sport-Kwest Trainers, you can slam-dunk the moon*, the commercials said. Looking at the moon right now, full and bright, Mark could almost believe it.

Of course, Mark wasn't dumb enough to think that a pair of shoes would turn him into a sports legend. But they had to be better than the dismal pair of no-name, shredded tennies he had now. Mom kept promising to replace them, but she just wanted to buy another bargain-bin pair. How could he even try out for the team with those on his feet? They'd laugh him off the court.

There was only one thing to do: Mark had to buy his own shoes. But at nearly two hundred bucks, snagging a pair of Sport-Kwest Trainers was about as likely as Mark slam-dunking the moon.

But Rudy had an idea. . . .

"Rich people are so greedy," Rudy had explained, "they like to take everything with them to the grave. Earrings, bracelets, diamond necklaces, you name it. I even heard about a guy who was buried in his Ferrari."

It was a foolproof plan, Rudy had said. Dig up jewelry that no one will miss and sell it on eBay. All Mark had to do was hold a flashlight and watch for guards. It sure beat six months of mowing lawns. At least that's what Mark had thought until he was there, at the cemetery fence.

"C'mon, what are you waiting for?" Rudy asked from the other side of the gates.

Mark looked up at the rusty iron sign above the gates. The *R* in *Rest* had broken, so the letters read PERPETUAL PEST MEMORIAL PARK.

Mark passed Rudy the flashlight through the bars. "You go on without me," Mark said. "I'll keep watch from out here."

"Forget it, dweeb," Rudy said, loud enough to maybe wake the dead, or at least the neighbors. "Ya snooze, ya lose—da shoes!" Then he laughed at his own cleverness. "You gotta be strong to make it in this world, bro," Rudy said. "So climb the fence and let's do this. Show me how strong you are."

Awkwardly, Mark climbed the fence, the iron cross-struts hurting Mark's feet because of his worn-out soles.

"Hurry up," Rudy snapped. Rudy made everything look easy and seem reasonable—from climbing a ten-foot fence to an array of criminal activities. Mark wondered if his brother's influence would land him in juvie, too, one day. Like maybe tomorrow.

"About time," said Rudy as Mark dropped from the fence, nearly spraining an ankle. "Here, take the shovel. I'll find the grave."

"You mean you have one in mind?"

"I do my research," Rudy said, like he was talking about a school project.

He started off into the graveyard, under a twisted canopy of trees. Ground fog swirled around him, like a ghostly sea. Mark took a deep breath and hurried after him, not really wanting to, but not wanting to be alone, either.

Up ahead, Rudy's flashlight beam bounced over the grounds of the cemetery, picking out marble headstones and vases stuffed with wilting flowers. Shadows danced with every step, like dark, scurrying animals. Mark heard the howl of a coyote—at least, he *hoped* it was a coyote—and smelled the sweet warmth of fresh-turned earth.

Mark tried to catch up with his brother, ignoring the gloom pressing in around him like cold tentacles in the mist. The graveyard was alive with unsettling sounds: the chirping of bugs, the hissing breath of the wind between headstones, the mysterious *scratch, scratch, scratch* of something unseen, like undead fingers, scrabbling upward through raw dirt. . . . Mark shook his head, furious at his own imagination.

"Wait up, Rudy!" But his brother wasn't listening. Rudy made a sharp turn, then came to a dead stop.

"We're here," he said.

They had come to an elaborate grave marked by an imposing statue of a mean-looking woman seated on a pedestal. If you looked real close, under the watery moonlight, you could see that the statue's teeth were bared, and its fingers splayed like claws.

A plaque resting at the foot of the statue read:

MADAME VORACIA THORNHILL
(1898–1962)
"Mine is yesterday, I know tomorrow."
—The Egyptian Book of the Dead

"Pretty creepy," said Mark.

"Creepy and *loaded*," Rudy said. "Mrs. Thornhill was married four times, and all of her husbands were filthy rich. They all died in suspicious ways. John Thornhill—her last husband's brother—swore she was a murderess. He broke into Thornhill Manor one night and shot her dead."

Rudy bent forward, lowering his voice. "After he killed her, John Thornhill was sent to a nuthouse. He kept saying his brother's wife wasn't human, that she was some kind of monster."

"Do you think—" Mark's voice broke. "Do you think it was true?"

"The guy was insane, dummy." Rudy grinned, reaching for the shovel. "But ya gotta love 'im, because what a gift he left for us!" He dug into the ground, pulling up a mound of moist earth. "Now hold that flashlight steady."

It took more than two hours.

By that time, Rudy was exhausted. Mark tried to help a couple of times, but his older brother kept saying he was too slow, and grabbing the shovel back. Soon sweat was dripping from Rudy's forehead in spite of the cold, and his breathing was ragged and hoarse. Still, he wouldn't give up. He just kept on shoveling, like a prisoner digging for freedom.

"You'll get your shoes," Rudy said as he dug, "and I'll get enough money to get away from here forever."

"Away where?"

Rudy didn't share the details of his final destination.

Then, just when it seemed Rudy might be ready to give up, the shovel went *CLUNK!* against something firm and hollow-sounding.

Rudy scraped the dirt aside, revealing a smooth curve of dull, faded mahogany.

"Pay dirt," Rudy said, which Mark noted was a weirdly appropriate expression.

From then on, it went quickly. Rudy dug furiously, and in less than ten minutes he'd cleared enough dirt to expose Madame Thornhill's coffin lid. It was scraped from Rudy's frantic digging, but still impressive: a large custom casket, as solid as the day it was laid to rest.

Rudy hunched down and gripped the lid with both hands. "Ready for the unveiling?"

"I don't know," said Mark, the flashlight unsteady in his hands. "Maybe this wasn't such a good idea—"

"Too late now." Rudy threw the coffin lid wide.

Mark gasped.

Madame Thornhill's body was shriveled like a mummy's; the eyes had collapsed in their sockets. Even her fancy gown was decaying.

But that wasn't the worst of it. The worst was that Madame Thornhill did not seem entirely human.

For one thing, the dead woman's hands were wrong. They were bent back at the wrist, with stubby fingers and sharp, curving fingernails. Mark had heard that a dead person's fingernails kept growing sometimes—but not like these. These were the claws of an animal.

But weirder still was her face.

Madame Thornhill's nose—well, it wasn't really a nose, it was more like a *snout*, stretching her dry cheeks like taffy. Huge canine teeth poked between papery lips.

"Rudy, let's get out of here," said Mark. "Now."

But Rudy hadn't seen the face and didn't notice the claws. His attention was on a necklace glimmering with jewels. "Those are diamonds!" said Rudy. "I knew it!"

Mark didn't care about the diamonds, the Sport-Kwest Trainers, or anything anymore. He just wanted to get as far from Perpetual Rest as he could.

"Rudy!"

"Shut up! I've almost got the clasp."

The clasp came undone, but the moment it did, the heavy necklace slid right into a hole in the center of Madame Thornhill's chest.

Mark could only shudder.

"Gross!" said Rudy. But it didn't stop him from reaching into her shattered rib cage to fish the thing out. He found it quickly and lifted it up. The diamonds glimmered in the moonlight.

"Okay, you got it," said Mark. "*Now* can we get the heck out of here?"

"Wait," said Rudy, frowning. "I think there's other stuff in there. . . . Whatever it is, it's shiny." Then he reached back into the dead woman's dry, dusty rib cage.

Mark realized what that shiny stuff must have been even before Rudy pulled it out.

Rudy looked at what he had in his hands and puzzled over it. "Freaky," he said. "These must be the bullets that killed her."

"Let me see them! Hurry!"

Rudy reached up and handed Mark the bullets. It was just as Mark had suspected. These weren't any old bullets that had put this woman to rest.

"Rudy, these are *silver* bullets!"

"Really? Do you think they're worth something?"

Rudy still didn't get the big picture, but to Mark it was as crystal clear as the full moon above them. You don't waste silver bullets on human beings. You save them for werewolves.

Mark dropped the bullets into his jacket pocket and desperately reached out to grab his brother's hand.

"Come out of there, Rudy! Come out now!"

But Rudy took his time, admiring the diamond necklace in his hand. "Well," he said proudly, "our work is done here."

Mark tried to warn his brother, but he was suddenly unable to speak, dry-mouthed with fear.

Because Madame Thornhill was beginning to move.

Rudy realized it a moment too late. He looked down and saw life returning to the creature's sunken eyeballs, saw its upper lip twitch like a dog sniffing a steak. Rudy might have escaped if he'd scrambled away in the next instant, while Madame Thornhill's old, dead limbs were swelling and flexing with recovered life. But he just stood there, frozen in disbelief—

And then it was too late.

The werewolf sprang at him with a snarl. Rudy went down under a flurry of teeth and claws, screaming. Mark saw nothing else, because he panicked and ran, dropping the flashlight. It bounced and fell into the open grave, throwing crazy shadows as Rudy fought for his life and lost, his screams quickly fading. Rudy was dead. And the wolf was still hungry.

Mark looked back only once and saw something he'd never forget, not if he lived to be a hundred, which right now seemed unlikely.

It was Madame Thornhill in stark silhouette, with her head thrown back and teeth bared, howling with such fury, it seemed to echo for miles. As Mark watched, the werewolf leaped out of its grave. With the silver bullets removed, its dry, ruined flesh was rapidly filling with life. Still shrouded in her shredded gown, Voracia Thornhill sniffed the air for game.

Her head swiveled toward him.

Mark ran.

There was nothing he could do for Rudy—he was dead. But maybe Mark could save himself. He knew he had only one chance to escape. Madame Thornhill might have been an ordinary woman without the light of a full moon, but now she was more animal than human—and there are things a human such as Mark can do that a wolf can't.

Like climb a ten-foot fence.

If Mark could make it to the edge of the cemetery and clear the fence before the werewolf caught him, he might survive! He had a head start of about thirty feet. But wolves are fast—you'd have to be a track star to outrun them.

Or a basketball star.

Mark tried to pretend he was on the court, driving the ball through the opposing line, blitzing toward the hoop with only seconds left on the clock. He tried not to think about the savage predator pounding toward him, its barbed teeth and wet tongue ready to gobble him down like raw hamburger. He could almost feel its hot breath on his shoulder, the sting of its razor claws. He ran, harder and faster than he ever had before.

The fence was right in front of him now. Mark jumped and caught the iron bars just as the back of his leg exploded in pain.

The werewolf had clamped its jaws down on his left calf. But Mark couldn't let the extraordinary pain in his leg, or the sight of his own blood, weaken him. He kicked at the creature's face with his other foot. It let go just long enough for Mark to pull himself up toward the top of the fence, ignoring the pain. The thing leaped at him again, but fell back down, unable to reach him. Mark felt dizzy and sick, but forced himself to keep climbing. He wedged a foot between the bars, shoved himself upward, and pulled with all his strength.

And then his foot got stuck.

He twisted and turned, trying to work it free. He couldn't. The bottom of his cheap, useless shoe had torn loose and was caught on a metal spur. In desperation, Mark grabbed one of the iron prongs at the top of the fence and tried to hoist himself up with it.

It broke off in his hand.

He fell.

And hit the ground at the werewolf's feet.

The creature stared down at him, drooling, its eyes gleaming with hunger. The werewolf looked ridiculous in Madame Thornhill's gown, but Mark wasn't laughing. He groped in his jacket pocket for the silver bullets, although he had no idea what to do with them.

Then the werewolf pounced.

Mark saw a quick flash of teeth like shredder blades. Because it didn't matter what he did now—no way would he live to see another sunrise—Mark did the only thing he could think of. He punched the werewolf.

His fist hit Voracia Thornhill in the chest and went deeper than he expected. Much deeper—because although the wolf was alive again, its wounds had not yet healed entirely. Mark's fist went through the hole in the monster's chest, and the werewolf shrieked like a dog in pain.

Instead of devouring him, the werewolf froze like a statue and crashed to the ground.

Mark realized why. In his clenched fist, now buried in the monster's chest cavity, he was holding the silver bullets. He'd clutched the bullets instinctively, so hard that his knuckles hurt, as if a part of him knew they were his last hope.

Gingerly, Mark opened his hand and pulled it free, leaving the bullets inside. The werewolf didn't stir. It was dead. Again. Re-dead, instead of un-dead.

He climbed the fence once more, this time much more carefully, and left Perpetual Rest Memorial Park.

They never found out how Rudy had died, and because no one knew that Mark had been there, he didn't have to explain.

The official story was that Rudy had joined a gang of vandals who had snuck into the cemetery. There was a fight, and Rudy was stabbed. Then coyotes must have gotten to him. Another body was found nearby, quickly identified as the remains of Madame Voracia Thornhill. No one could venture a guess as to how or why the body had been left at the cemetery fence.

Their mom was heartbroken over Rudy's death. But she'd be okay. She confessed to Mark that she'd always suspected Rudy would meet with an unhappy end. Rudy had always said he wanted out of here forever. In a way, Mark figured, Rudy had gotten exactly what he had asked for.

"You gotta be strong to make it in this world," Rudy had always told him. But you also had to be smart. Mark couldn't feel guilty that he was the one who'd survived. He had made it out alive and had even healed from a serious werewolf bite without anyone ever knowing.

Mark never got his Sport-Kwest Trainers, but he found he didn't need them. That night in the cemetery had done wonders for his self-confidence. If Mark could outrun a charging werewolf, surely he could handle a full-court press.

Besides, he'd checked next year's calendar. Four of the games would be played during a full moon.

Just try to stop him *then*.

GHOST DOG

by Ellen Wittlinger

"That's Hawkins," Travis told Jack, motioning to the elderly man sitting on his front porch. "Old guy's squirrelly." Travis raised a finger to his ear and circled it.

The two boys walked a little faster past the only other house on Reservoir Road besides the one Jack and his mother had moved into the week before. But Hawkins noticed them and pulled himself out of his rocking chair onto long, unsteady legs.

"Hey!" he called. "You seen my dog anywhere? She's gone missin'!"

Jack stopped and looked at the man. His grandma's dog had run away once, and the whole family had been upset until he came back.

"What's she look like?" Jack asked.

"Let's go!" Travis hissed. "Don't talk to Hawkins! You can't believe a word he says!"

But the old man was staring at Jack now. It wouldn't hurt to find out what the dog looked like. Maybe they'd see it while they were walking around.

"Black and white," Hawkins said. "'Bout so high." The flat of his hand measured the dog's height at halfway between his knee and his hip bone. Not a small animal. "She answers to the name Jessie."

Travis let out a sharp laugh. "I can't believe you're talking to this nut. Let's go!"

"I'll let you know if I see her," Jack told the old man.

"Thank you, son. Thank you." Hawkins sank back down into his chair, which groaned a warning. The rocker didn't seem sturdy enough to hold the man's thin frame; in fact, Jack thought, the whole house looked on the verge of collapse.

"Come on." Travis gave him a little shove to get him moving, and the two of them walked on down the road.

Jack wasn't sure what he thought of Travis—the boy was awfully bossy and had to have things his own way all the time. But he did know a lot about the local countryside, and it had been fun exploring the woods with him, something Jack had never done when he lived in the city. Besides, Travis was the only kid close to his age he'd seen since he'd moved here. At first Jack had been glad to find him, but the more time they spent together, the more Travis irked him. Why, for instance, did he have to be so mean to an old man who only wanted to find his lost dog?

Back in Chicago, Jack had had a friend who lived in the same building he did, and two more friends just down the street. But when they'd moved to Michigan, after his dad left, the only place his mom could afford was a house in the middle of nowhere. He hoped when school started he'd meet other kids, but for now, if he wanted somebody to hang out with, it would have to be Travis.

"Can't believe you talked to Hawkins," Travis said, shaking his head. "Now he's gonna want to talk to you all the time."

"He lost his dog. I thought I might be able to help," Jack said.

"Right. Lost his dog." Travis shook his head disdainfully. "Do you want to hear about how he 'lost' his dog? He *ran over* the dog with that old truck of his. That's right! He's never gonna find that dog again because Jessie is dead and it's his own fault!"

"Really?" Jack asked.

Travis walked backward in front of Jack, his eyes flashing. "Really. I wouldn't make up something like that."

"Wow, that's terrible. I bet that's why he's so crazy now."

"He deserves to be crazy. He killed his own dog!"

"But it was an accident, wasn't it? He didn't do it on purpose."

Travis turned away. "What I heard was, he was in a big hurry. Wasn't paying attention. Dog was just layin' there on the dirt driveway, and Hawkins drove right over her."

Jack shook his head. "Man, that's awful."

Travis was quiet for a minute, and then he said, "Some people say they've seen Jessie in the woods around Hawkins's old shack. Maybe she comes back to see him."

Jack's heart jumped in his chest, and he looked around him as if he might catch sight of the animal. He assured himself he wasn't really afraid; it was just that Travis was talking in a creepy voice, no doubt trying to scare him.

"I don't believe in stuff like that," Jack said. "No such thing as ghosts. Especially ghost *dogs*."

Travis shrugged. "I'm just saying what I heard."

They were both quiet until they reached the sidewalk in front of Jack's house.

"I should go," Travis said.

Jack figured Travis would stay if he invited him in, but he'd had enough of the boy for one afternoon. "Where do you live, anyway?"

Travis pointed through the trees. "Over that way. Off Dakota Road. There's a shortcut through the woods."

"Oh. Well, I guess I'll see you around."

Travis gave him a little wave and headed off through the trees.

At dinner that night, Jack's mother was on him again about making friends. She'd met a woman at her new job in the dentist's office who had a daughter his age, and she was plotting to get the two of them together.

"I'm not in kindergarten, Mom. You can't make playdates for me. Besides, a girl is not going to want to hang out with some guy she doesn't even know."

"I told her mother what a wonderful kid you are. I'm sure—"

"No, Mom. No, no, no."

She sighed. "But you need some friends, Jack."

"I have a friend. I told you."

"I know, Travis. I'd like to meet him sometime. Sounds like he doesn't have anything better to do than hang around in the woods all day."

"So? I don't have anything better to do, either." Jack knew he sounded angry.

His mother grimaced, then stared out the window, her eyes unfocused. "Maybe I shouldn't have moved you here. It was selfish of me. I wanted to be closer to my parents after . . . But I know it wasn't fair to you. You always liked Chicago so much."

"I'll go back. I'll see my friends when I visit Dad."

Jack knew that any mention of his father still had the power to make his mother fall apart. She left the table silently and retreated to her bedroom. Maybe that was what he'd wanted her to do. Leave him alone. Her constant commentary on how lousy his life was these days didn't make him feel any better about it.

The next day, after his mother left for work, Jack got on his bike and rode down Reservoir Road. Travis hadn't been around that morning, and Jack decided to go talk to Hawkins for a while. He couldn't get out of his head the story of how the man had accidentally killed his dog, and he felt sorry for the old guy. He wouldn't mind sitting and listening to Hawkins tell stories about Jessie—there was nothing else to do, anyway.

But before he got as far as Hawkins's cabin, he heard someone calling his name. It had to be Travis—he didn't know anybody else.

"Where are you?" He peered through the trees that lined the road.

"Over here," Travis said, whispering just loud enough for Jack to hear.

Jack let his bike drop and followed the sound of Travis's voice. He found the boy ten yards into the woods, crouching low to the ground. Travis held a finger to his lips.

"What's going on?" Jack whispered.

Travis pointed through the trees. "Get down! I see her. She's over there!"

Jack got on his knees and struggled to see whatever it was Travis saw, but there was nothing there, just trees and more trees. Although when he turned his head, he thought there might be something moving in his peripheral vision, something that didn't want to be seen head-on.

Then all of a sudden, there she was standing in the clearing. White face, black markings on her back, long pink tongue lolling from one corner of her mouth.

"That's her! That's Jessie!" Travis said. "The ghost dog!"

Jack's skin prickled. Was it possible? The dog stared at him, looking as real and solid as any dog he'd ever seen. And then he figured it out: This was Travis's idea of a joke. He wanted Jack to go screaming out of the woods, scared to death, so that when school started, he could tell everybody what a sissy Jack was, afraid of ghosts. Well, that was not going to happen.

"Just looks like a regular old dog to me," Jack said, standing up.

"Stay down, you idiot!" Travis whispered. "She wasn't that friendly even when she was alive. Bein' run over probably didn't make her any nicer."

"That dog's no more a ghost than I am," Jack said. He left Travis's side and began to walk confidently into the clearing, where the dog stood glaring at him.

"You don't know a darn thing about ghosts!" Travis called after him. "Jessie'll take your leg off!"

And, in fact, Jessie, or whoever the dog was, bared her teeth as

Jack approached. He could hear a low growl begin in the animal's throat and work its way up. Jack knew it probably wasn't the smartest thing to do to approach a strange dog in the woods. Ghost or not, the mutt didn't look too happy to see him. Still, he couldn't let Travis make a fool of him.

He put a hand out tentatively. The dog took a step back and rolled up her lip so her teeth showed. "Hey, doggie," Jack said. "Are you a ghost? You don't look like you got run over by a—" But before he could finish his sentence, the dog leaped for him, and not for his leg, either. For his throat.

Without thinking, Jack tried to block the dog with his arm and felt the furious animal's teeth sink through the flesh of his shoulder. The sudden pain would have dropped him to his knees in any other situation, but fear kept him on his feet. He tried his best to pull away, but the dog held tight.

"Jessie! Let him go!" Travis ran at the dog, waving his arms. "Back off, Jessie. Go away!"

To Jack's surprise, Jessie let go. Travis stomped his feet at her, and the dog backed away, licking her lips, then turned and ran off into the woods.

"I told you not to go after her!" Travis said. "What did you think she'd do, roll over and give you a kiss?"

Jack cradled his bitten arm with his good arm and staggered back out to the road, Travis following him. "That was no ghost dog, Travis. That was a living, breathing, crazy animal."

Travis rolled his eyes. "And how do you know that?"

"Because ghosts don't have teeth! Ghosts don't bite you and make you bleed!"

"You're not bleeding," Travis said matter-of-factly. "Your shirt isn't even ripped."

"What?" Jack stopped walking and looked down at his arm. Sure enough, there was no trace of a dog bite, not even a scratch.

"I felt her bite me," Jack said. "It hurt!" But, oddly enough, his arm didn't seem to hurt anymore; the pain had disappeared with the dog.

Travis shrugged, then smiled. "You look like you saw a ghost."

When Jack's mother got home from work, she found him sitting on the couch staring out the window.

"You've got the funniest look on your face," she said. "What are you thinking about?"

He decided to come right out and ask her. "Do you believe in ghosts?"

She flopped down onto the couch, next to him. "Like Halloween ghosts?"

"No, like dead people who aren't totally dead. Or maybe even dead dogs that you can still see."

She sighed and shook her head. "Oh, Jack. It's living so far out in the sticks that's made you think about ghosts, isn't it? Spending the whole day here alone. You're scaring yourself with this silly stuff."

"Maybe it isn't silly. You know that old guy, Hawkins, who lives down the road?"

"*Mister* Hawkins, Jack. You know better than to call an elderly man by his last name."

"*Mister* Hawkins. He had this dog that he ran over with his truck, and the dog died. But I saw it today in the woods."

"What do you mean, you saw it?"

"Travis saw it first and called me over, but I saw it, too."

She chuckled. "I think this Travis friend of yours has a vivid imagination. You have more sense than to believe something like that, Jack."

"Mom, listen to me! The dog bit me, here, on my arm—"

Jack's mother grabbed his arm. "A dog *bit* you? You should have called me right away. You need to get a tetanus shot!" She turned his arm over in her hand. "Where did the dog bite you? I don't see anything."

"It went away. At first it hurt like anything, and then it just disappeared."

"Oh, for Pete's sake." She let his arm drop back to his side. "If you're trying to scare me, it won't work. I grew up around here, and I've heard every dumb story these local farmers can make up. Ghost dogs. That's a good one. Go wash your hands and help me make dinner."

On the one hand, Jack was glad to hear his mother say it couldn't possibly have happened, that he'd somehow made it all up. On the other hand, he knew he'd seen that dog. And felt that bite.

The following morning, Travis was waiting for him on the road in front of his house.

"Wanna go look for Jessie again?" he said.

"No. I'm going to go talk to Mr. Hawkins," Jack said.

"Why do you wanna talk to him?" Travis said. "Old fool don't know if it's midnight or Tuesday."

"Well, that's where I'm going."

Travis looked annoyed. "Fine, while you're listening to him jabber, I'm gonna look for Jessie out back of his place."

"Whatever."

They walked up the road quickly, as if they had jobs to do. When they came in sight of Mr. Hawkins's shack, Travis turned into the woods.

"I'll call you if I find her."

"I don't wanna see that dog again, Travis. She bit me, remember?"

"Where?" Travis said. "I don't see no bite." He laughed as he disappeared among the trees.

Mr. Hawkins was sitting on his front porch as usual. As Jack approached, the old man recognized him. Leaning forward in his rocker, he called, "You find my dog? My Jessie?"

Jack came to the bottom of the porch stairs. "That's what I wanted to talk to you about. I think I did see her."

Mr. Hawkins slapped his knee and grinned; he was short a few teeth. "I *knew* she'd come back. Where was she? In the woods? She always did like to run off in them woods."

Jack nodded. "Yeah, in the woods. But I wanted to ask you something. I know it sounds weird, but, Mr. Hawkins, is that dog alive?"

The smile wavered on his face as Mr. Hawkins sank back into his chair. "What do you mean, is she alive? You saw her, didn't you? You said you saw her."

"I know. I did see her. But somebody told me that . . ." Jack paused and took a deep breath. How did you ask a person a question like that? Just straight out, he guessed. "I heard that you ran over

Jessie with your truck. Accidentally. And . . . she died."

Mr. Hawkins said nothing. His gaze left Jack's face and settled on his own hands where they rested on his chest. Finally, he took a deep breath and shuddered as he let it out. "I would never hurt my Jessie girl. I love that old dog."

Jack nodded. "I know. But can you remember if an accident like that might have happened?"

"Might have," Mr. Hawkins said, his head cocked oddly to the side, his voice low and hoarse. "I remember one time I got in my truck and I was real late. Supposed to meet my wife in town. Not paying attention . . ." He seemed to drift off into his own thoughts.

"When was that?" Jack asked, just to keep the man talking.

Mr. Hawkins shrugged his sagging shoulders. "Maybe fifteen years ago. My wife, Selma, was still alive."

Fifteen years ago? That couldn't have been when he hit Jessie. Travis had seen the dog alive, and Travis couldn't be more than twelve.

Suddenly, Mr. Hawkins sat erect as if he'd been struck by lightning; then, just as quickly, he collapsed back into the chair, his head falling into his hands. "Oh, Lordy, why didn't I look behind me? Why didn't I pay attention? God forgive me!"

Jack felt so sorry for the old man that he walked up onto the porch to put a hand on his arm. "It was an accident, Mr. Hawkins. You didn't know the dog was there."

Mr. Hawkins looked up at Jack with tears running down his cheeks. "Didn't know *neither* of 'em was there. That boy loved Jessie so much, he'd come over and lie down in the dirt with her. Weren't no kids around here—Jessie was his only friend. I ran over 'em both, boy and dog. They was dead before the ambulance got here, Lord forgive me!"

Jack's whole body began to shake. He reminded himself that Mr. Hawkins was a crazy old man who probably didn't know what he was saying. Still, Jack had to ask.

"What boy, Mr. Hawkins? What was his name?"

The old man sniffed back his tears and looked at the woods. "Name was Travis. Lived over off Dakota Road, through the woods, but he came here to see Jessie every day."

Jack backed away from Mr. Hawkins, stumbling on the top step and almost falling backward. "That's not true! You're trying to trick me, both of you!"

From behind him, Jack heard a voice say, "Now, why would I want to trick you?" When he turned around, there stood Travis with the black-and-white dog sitting calmly next to him. "Seemed like you didn't have any friends," Travis continued, looking just the same as he had for the last week, a half smile curling up his mouth. "If you want to play with us, I'll tell Jessie not to bite you anymore."

"Stop it!" Jack cried. "You can't be dead! You can't!"

"I'm not dead," Mr. Hawkins said. "Close to it, probably, but not dead yet."

"Not you, him!" Jack said, pointing to Travis. "He's standing right there with Jessie!"

Mr. Hawkins looked where Jack was pointing. "Son, I think you been out in the sun too long. You need a drink o' water?" The old man stood up slowly from his chair.

But Jack had already leaped from the porch stairs to the sidewalk and backed off onto the grass. "Go away, Travis! Leave me alone!"

And then, to Mr. Hawkins's surprise, he turned and ran.

"Being alone is no fun," Travis yelled after him. "When you get lonely, we'll be waiting for you in the woods!"

Jack tried not to hear him. He ran fast down Reservoir Road until he came to his own small house surrounded by woods in the middle of nowhere.

GOING OLD SCHOOL IN THE AGE OF OBAMA

by Christopher Paul Curtis

Half an hour to the bell.

So it's Friday, and I'm sitting here in third-period English, stressing. Fourth period is phys ed and Friday is dodgeball day. That's where Mr. Williams, the gym teacher/coach/chief-psychotic-maniac-adult at McKinley Middle School, divides the class into two teams. And—surprise!—it always works out to be his athletes, who he calls "The Men," against the rest of us, the pencil-neck-geekish-nerds, or "The Penguins." Which is a name that's way too clever for Coach to have come up with on his own. I wonder who helped him?

Here's another shocker: The captain of The Men's dodgeball team always turns out to be Darnell Antoine Wilson, the quarterback/point guard/chief-psychotic-maniac-student at the school, or, as we Penguins call him, The Arm of Thor. Darnell Antoine Wilson throws those big rubber balls so hard that they flatten out as they come rocketing at you. They don't go *WHOOOOSH!* They sound more like a jet engine taking off.

Coach Williams considerately chooses Fridays as dodgeball day 'cause that gives us Penguins the whole weekend to recover from our wounds.

Twenty-five minutes to the bell.

You gotta give Darnell credit. He's invented his own special system to mow us nerds down. He doesn't just blast any-old-body any-old-way. Somewhere in that reptilian brain of his, he's come up with a certain order that he follows. He's broken us Penguins into three groups.

The first group he goes after is The Penguins With Glasses. He tries to see how far he can make their glasses fly. His record is an estimated thirty-two feet. Coach Williams could only estimate it because Jerry Goldberg's glasses are still hanging from the rafters of the gym, an estimated thirty-two feet away.

His next victims are the ones who, as soon as Coach Williams blows the whistle, curl up in little balls and start whining. Darnell's goal is to see how many Curling Whiners he can ricochet off of with one shot. Sort of like he's shooting pool, or bowling. He once bounced Eddie Patrick into four kids who were cowering behind Eddie, and they all went down.

The last group of Penguins is the one I'm in. We're known as The Idiots. We actually put up a fight . . . sometimes. We've been known to every-once-in-a-while actually throw the ball back at Darnell and The Men. There used to be three of us—me, Lenny Ucci, and Little Marvy Ware—but Little Marvy transferred over to the Curling Whiners after throwing a ball that Darnell caught in his teeth and blew to bits by biting. The smell of stale rubber mingled with the smell of unwashed boys in the gym for days.

Twenty minutes to the bell.

I guess in some ways we Penguins are lucky, because we *are* involved in greatness. I think it might've been Martin Luther King who said something about trying to be the best at whatever you do. You know, if you're a janitor, try to be the best janitor out there, or, if you're a garbage collector, be the best one in town. Or, in Darnell Antoine Wilson's case, if you're gonna be a bully, be the best bully anyone has ever seen. That's Darnell—he's always amping up his bullying skills, always coming up with something new.

On dodgeball Fridays, he's not happy simply shifting your major organs around in your body. He's only satisfied if you hobble away with lasting psychological scars, too.

This year he's been having Theme Days. Every Friday, he announces what that game's theme is. When he hits the last person in one of the three groups of Penguins, he busts out some stale insult joke.

Last week's theme was "Ugliness." Just before he bruised the kidneys of the final Penguin With Glasses, he told him, "You're so ugly, I took you to the zoo, and the zookeeper said, 'Thanks for bringing him back!' " The week before that's theme was "Stupidity." Right before the last Curling Whiner wound up under the bleachers, Darnell said to him, "You're so stupid, you opened a box of Cheerios and said, 'Look, donut seeds!' "

I chew deeper into where my thumbnail used to be, and wonder what today's theme is going to be.

Fifteen minutes to the bell.

So, like I said, I'm sitting here, stressing, wondering if I should leave The Idiots and let Lenny Ucci stand alone. Wondering if maybe I could get some fake glasses, so at least I'd be put out of my misery early on.

Why me? Why me?

My hands are shaking so much that I reach over and grab my left wrist to slow it down. That's when the answer comes to me—when I feel my blue rubber wristband that has w.w.G.L.D. printed on it.

Okay, Maurice, I tell myself. *Chill. Think this through. Try to figure out: "What Would Grampa Lefty Do?"*

I'm not bragging, but I've got some pretty special roots, and not one of my ancestors would put up with this. I'm from a long line of people who used to strike terrifying fear into the souls of other folks, and all I've got to do is get my mind right and borrow some of their spine.

I rub the blue rubber wristband and feel myself getting stronger and stronger. More and more confident. Less and less afraid.

I start thinking like the old folks did. I start looking at the whole situation in a new way.

The first thing that comes to my mind is that Darnell Antoine Wilson is asking for it. And, when I say that, I don't mean he's quietly begging for help, either. It's like he's standing on top of the tallest building in downtown Flint, Michigan, screaming at the top of his lungs, "Could someone please show me how big a buster I am?"

I gotta tell you, with my new attitude, I'm the one who can point it out to him.

Even though this goes against everything Moms and Pops taught me since I was old enough to understand the difference between the folks in my ethnic group and those in Darnell's, and even yours.

My parents say, "Maurice, you've got to be better than them. You've got to do your part to fight all the stereotypes they believe about us. You've got to be twice as kind, twice as compassionate, and twice as understanding as they are." But that isn't real. I try to deal with the real.

"Sweetheart," Moms says, "things have changed. You're living in the age of Obama now. You've got to be willing to reach out to all kinds of people."

Blah-blah-blah.

My parents are as old as mud, and I hate to break the news to them, but here in the real world of middle school, kindness, compassion, and understanding ain't exactly on the menu. As for reaching out? All that'll get you is CPR and an ambulance ride to the hospital.

Ten minutes to the bell.

You can call me prejudiced, but I know your people aren't ever gonna welcome people from my ethnic group into your new global village. By "your people," I mean you single-hyphes—those of you with only one hyphen in your names. Like the Asian-Americans, the Native-Americans, the European-Americans, the Hispanic-Americans, the African-Americans, and so on and so on and so on.

My people are the *double*-hyphes—we've got two hyphens in our names. We're the Vamp-Asian-Americans, the Vamp-Native-Americans, the Vamp-European-Americans, the Vamp-Hispanic-Americans—and my crew, the Vamp-African-Americans.

That's right. We're the ones you used to call the V-word. We're Vampires.

Not so willing to invite me over for a night of Guitar Hero now, are you? Though I can't say I really blame you for feeling that way, 'cause you've been brainwashed and taught nothing but nonsense about us since you were little.

The biggest lie is that we need fresh human blood to live—what we double-hyphes call the "Vee Vant To Bite You On Da Neck" lie. I'm not denying it—there's no shame in my game—we do need a shot of human blood every once in a while. But that doesn't mean we're gonna go through the hassle of hiding in the bushes, waiting to wrestle some single-hyphe to get our fill.

Think about it.

When you want a hamburger, you don't run down to Farmer Brown's, jump the fence, and bite one of his cows on the butt, do you? Of course not. Just like when we want to get our feed on, we don't go over to Wal-Mart and chomp down on one of those greeter dudes. *Everybody* gets their food processed these days. You go to the grocery store or Burger King. We got our own little fast-food joints, too.

Even five-year-old Vamp-American kids learn about that in Vampire History classes. Our ancient leader, Grampa Lefty, wrote that way back in 1921, the great Vamp-Native-American inventor Jay "One-Thumb" Kicknowsway came up with a way to preserve human blood without using all the toxic chemicals the Red Cross does. Since 1922 we've been buying our blood supplements. The last known case of a Vampire actually biting a single-hyphe was back in the Great Depression. But will you people let us forget that?

Not likely.

Haven't you ever wondered why there are so many blood banks downtown? My uncle Tyrone owns five of them right here in Flint.

Five minutes to the bell.

There's another fairy tale you people have made up about us. That if you drive a wooden stake into our hearts while we're asleep, it'll kill us.

Duh.

Yeah, last time I checked, pounding a sharp stick through my chest will do me in. But so will running me over with your momma's Hummer, dropping a radio in my bathwater, or sprinkling my cornflakes with arsenic. Those are all one-way tickets to Vampire Heaven, too.

Then there's the myth that if we bite one of you single-hyphes, either you'll die from blood loss, or, worse than that, you'll become one of us. Come on—we're not pigs. A half-pint of blood will fill up the biggest Vamp-American for weeks. And no one dies from being bitten. There are supposed to be certain attitude changes that happen after a Vampire bite, but that's to be expected—having someone bite you is real personal and helps you see more clearly what's what. As for becoming a Vampire afterward? That's just like everything else in life—you're either born a Vampire or you're not. Get over yourselves. No one's looking to recruit you.

Two minutes to the bell.

How about the lie that all Vampires are European? We learned during Vampire History Week that there have been 12,541 films made about Vamp-European-Americans, and only one about a Vamp-African-American—*Blacula*. What an embarrassment that flick is. Afros? Bell-bottoms? Polyester capes?

Gimme a break.

Besides that, have you ever looked at the neck of your average middle schooler? Biting it ain't the first thing that comes to mind, is it? I bet there's more funk and bacteria growing on Darnell's neck than in any sewer in Flint. And you honestly think me and my people are looking to bite there?

Please.

The more I think about it, the madder I get. I'm mad about the way people like Darnell Antoine Wilson and other single-hyphes have been treating my people for centuries. Mad to think that I've been so scared that I always back down from him and his type. And with anger comes strength. Darnell has messed over me for the last time in this life. I'm gonna reach into my roots and go Old School on him.

The bell explodes into my thoughts, but doesn't knock a bit of my newfound courage aside.

I change into my shorts and T-shirt and walk into the gym. I'm totally locked in on what I'm going to do to Darnell. I can see the respect the other Penguins will have in their eyes once I destroy our tormentor—the same respect I'll see in myself in the mirror.

The Men and Coach Williams stand on one side of the gym, and The Penguins huddle on the other.

Just like every other Friday, Coach sets six balls on the half-court line, and, just like every other Friday, that's the sign for The Penguins to start moaning and whimpering. Just like every other Friday, the whistle blows, and no one but Darnell Antoine Wilson moves.

He calmly strolls to half-court and picks up his first ball.

Just like every other Friday, The Penguins who don't wear glasses instinctively move away from the five who do.

Darnell Antoine Wilson says, "Okay, Penguins, you're lucky. This afternoon is all about 'Poperty.'"

Lenny Ucci grabs my arms and says, "What? I don't think my

hearing has come all the way back from last Friday—did he say it's Property Day? What on earth can that be about?"

After Darnell blasts four Penguins, Jerry Goldberg knows he's the last. He's tied a string to the end of his glasses so that when he comes to, he'll be able to pull them back from wherever they landed.

Darnell says, "Jerry Goldberg, you're so poor that if someone tried to rob you, he'd just be practicing!"

Oh! I see—what Professor Darnell Antoine Wilson was trying to say was that it's Poverty Day!

He winds up and throws. The ball forms itself around Jerry's head so perfectly and so quickly that his glasses don't even move. Jerry topples to the floor and bounces three times before he finally comes to a rest.

Coach Williams and The Men cheer.

Darnell finishes off four Curling Whiners and has only Little Marvy Ware left.

"Marvin Ware," he shouts, "you're so poor, you go to McDonald's and put a milk shake on layaway."

Little Marvy knocks down only two people before he smashes into the back wall.

Darnell must be having an off day.

Next, it's gonna be me or Lenny Ucci.

Darnell's eyes lock on Lenny.

Great—I get to watch everyone else's pain before Darnell closes the show with me.

Darnell jumps about four feet in the air, does a 360, and, before his body comes back down, launches the ball at Lenny.

He *was* having an off day. Instead of hitting Lenny in the face, where Darnell always aims, the ball catches Lenny in his left knee.

I think it must be an optical illusion—for a moment, Lenny's whole left leg, from the hip down, just vanishes.

Darnell knocked Lenny's leg clean off!

But no—a split second later, we all see Lenny's left leg, still attached, as his sneaker flies off and knocks him square on the side of his head. Lenny yelps like a stepped-on Chihuahua and drags his left leg behind him like a gigantic Polish sausage wearing a sock. Then he pogo-sticks on his right leg out the gym door.

The Men go wild!

My heart sinks as they start chanting, "You can't top that! You can't top that! You can't top that!"

Great. Egg Darnell on to new levels of cruelty!

That's when the voices of the taunting Men fade away, and all I can hear is the voice of our great leader. Grampa Lefty.

"Son," he whispers, "throw with all your might. Throw the ball, and your ancestors will guide you, will strengthen you, will strike this hoodlum down with a vengeance unknown to single-hyphes since the Middle Ages!"

I pick up the ball. I can't believe it. It's actually hot!

I ignore the burning pain in my hands. I rev my arm back. I feel the power of my ancestors course through my body. I grunt mightily and let the ball fly.

I guess I must come from a long line of Penguins.

The stupid ball bounces twice before it gently bumps Darnell's sneaker. He smiles, bends over, and picks it up.

"Maurice Bledsoe," Darnell Antoine Wilson says, "you're so poor, the folks from Goodwill leave roadkill on your front lawn to help y'all out with food!"

Blessedly, darkness immediately follows.

The first of your senses to return after you're knocked out is your hearing. I can tell I've been moved to the locker room because I can hear the *drip-drip-drip* of the showers. I also hear someone singing off-key. It sounds like Darnell.

The next sense to come back is smell. I inhale deeply. Yup, the locker room.

I feel something hard press into my back. Oh. They've laid me out on the benches between the lockers.

Finally my eyes open. I have to blink a couple of times, because someone's standing over me, looking down. I blink harder. I guess Darnell has come to finish me off.

But—no. This person is much older and has a much kinder face.

Wait a minute. I recognize this dude from the cover of my Vampire History book.

"Grampa Lefty?"

This can't be good. Some psychopathic single-hyphe drove a stake into Grampa Lefty during his afternoon nap back in the 1930s.

But it *is* him.

He says, "Yes, my son."

I swallow hard and ask, "Does seeing you mean I'm . . ."

He smiles. "No, Maurice, I'm not an angel of death. I usually reveal myself only to those who are most in need of my advice."

Whew!

"So I'm not dead . . . I just need a little advice?"

Grampa Lefty says, "Well, you could use *lots* of advice, but that's not why I'm here."

"Huh?"

"I'm here to do something I haven't done since 1922. I give you permission to take care of that clown right there."

Grampa Lefty points a long, dark brown, crooked finger at the other end of the bench. Darnell Antoine Wilson is sitting there, singing, pulling his socks on.

"*What?*" I say.

Grampa Lefty says, "For the first time in nearly ninety years, I'm granting my permission for one of my peeps to bite someone on the neck."

I may be semiconscious, but the thought of biting Darnell's nasty neck makes me nearly gag. "But, Grampa Lefty," I say, "we're living in the age of Obama now."

He says, "What's right is right, and there ain't one thing right about that boy. Let's see if there might be an attitude readjustment with that jerk after you're done. Take care of him, now. You can start living in the age of Obama in about ten minutes."

I gulp and ask, "Is that an order?"

He smiles and starts fading away. The last thing he says is "There's a bottle of Listerine in Jerry Goldberg's locker. He won't mind if you borrow it."

I stand up. I walk behind where Darnell Antoine Wilson is leaning over, tying his sneaker. I tap him on the shoulder and, just like that, bite my way into Vampire History.

ANASAZI BREAKDOWN

by Douglas Rees

The wind blew cold across the desert, rattling the dry brush. To Darcy Williams, it sounded like old bones trying to knit together. She pushed the image away. Darcy didn't care for nonsense. And her real problems were bad enough. She didn't need to invent new fears.

Cold, Darcy thought. *How can a desert be so cold?*

It had been warm all day, and the New Mexico sun had been as bright as one of the shiny aluminum birds her mother kept buying in gift shops. The sun had glared down on the walls of the ancient stone ruins that filled Chaco Canyon. The rocks became blazing hot, making the black lines on the pale piece of pottery she found stand out like spells written in a strange language. The lines on the potsherd—this fragment—ran from one edge of the big, curving arch of clay to the other. And they called to her.

Darcy had stopped in her tracks when she saw this broken piece of pot. Automatically, she had looked around to see where her mother was, to see if she was watching. Perhaps Darcy had decided what she was going to do before she had formed the idea.

Yes, her mother was a quarter of a mile off. More important, she was looking away from Darcy, taking another photo of another ruined wall with its strange T-shaped doorway. In a flash, Darcy had bent down, snatched up the piece of pot, and tucked it inside her shirt.

She knew this was illegal. There were signs everywhere that said so. She understood why tourists were forbidden to take the ancient artifacts that lay under their feet. The place an object is found in can tell a great deal about it. Take it away from its spot, and you can destroy most of the story it had to tell. That was science, and Darcy respected science.

The clay fragment was the first thing she had stolen in her life.

It hadn't been from boredom, or because of a sudden whim to take something for the fun of it. Darcy had done it for love. Her mother had always wanted to make this trip. To see the mesas and deep skies of the Colorado Plateau, and to visit the Anasazi ruins. Darcy's mother and father had planned the trip over and over. When the day came that her father was no longer sick, they would go there, the three of them.

Some nights, Darcy and her father had sat together looking at photographs of the high, wild land, and of the ruins. Always, the ruins. Darcy could remember her father telling her, "Nobody knows who built them, Darcy. Nobody knows why they put them where they did, or why they left. But out in the middle of this desert, people came together and created houses of stones. They built them three, four stories high. They constructed them on the sides of cliffs and on canyon floors. There were thousands of people, and they lived there for hundreds of years. Then—they left. Nobody knows where they went. And this wasn't in some foreign country thousands of miles away. It was right here in America, and we can drive out there and see it all. Someday we will. A good, long trip."

Then, always, he had coughed without stopping. Darcy's mother had to help him to bed.

During one of his last days, her father had made his wife promise that she and Darcy would do what he couldn't do. And when the funeral was over and all the mourners had left, Darcy and her mother loaded up the large pickup truck and went.

So Darcy had taken the potsherd to give to her mother at Christmas. Her mother would open the box lined with special purple paper that Darcy knew would set off its colors. She would see the elegant curve of clay and gasp, and confusion would cross her face. Then she would look up at Darcy, realize what she had done, and why she had done it.

"Darcy, you shouldn't have," she would say.

"I shouldn't have, but I did," Darcy would reply. "Merry Christmas, Mom."

And her mother would cry, and Darcy would know that she had given her mother the perfect gift.

That was what she'd been imagining when she placed her foot wrong and fell.

My pot! Darcy thought as she went down. She cried out as she twisted, trying to fall on her side, to protect the pot. She landed hard and felt something go wrong with her knee.

When she tried to get up, she couldn't stand upright. She bent over, like someone very old. Her shadow reminded her of a bird with a broken wing.

Her mother was already running to her. She put her arms around Darcy and tried to help her straighten up, but that only made Darcy scream with pain. Slowly, one step at a time, Darcy limped to the truck and crawled into the backseat.

The road that led to Chaco Canyon was unpaved and empty. It ran twenty miles to link up with the highway to Nageezi. Darcy's mother tried to drive a steady thirty, the speed at which the dirt road was smoothest. Even so, Darcy was moaning in discomfort. Probably that was why her mother didn't see the coyote that ran in front of the truck until it was too late.

They felt the thump even while Darcy's mother slammed on the brakes, sending Darcy nearly off the seat and into a spasm of pain.

Her mother got out. She walked around the front of the truck, holding high over her head a metal bar, the one she used for locking the steering wheel.

"Nothing!" Darcy heard her mother say.

"But we saw it. We *felt* it," Darcy said through her teeth. "We must've hit it."

"Then it probably limped off into the brush," her mother said. "But I don't see any blood. I don't see *anything*. Well, I've got more important things to worry about. Let's get you to a hospital."

She got back into the truck and turned the key.

Nothing.

It wasn't the battery. The truck's lights still worked. The dials on the dashboard sprang to life as soon as the key turned. But the truck wouldn't start.

"Maybe it's a vapor lock," Darcy's mother said. "If we just sit a while, it may fix itself."

It didn't. And the dirt road stayed empty.

Darcy's mother tried her cell phone, but there was no service. At last, when the sun was well past its high point, she said, "There's no way you can walk."

"I know, Mom."

"I have to leave, Darcy. I've got to go for help. There's no telling how long it'll be before someone drives down this road. And even if they do, they may not stop. I'll have to walk to that little town. I'm sorry, but there's no other way." There were tears in her eyes.

"I know, Mom," Darcy said again. "Don't worry. I'll be okay. It's not like there's anyone out here."

"Just stay inside and keep the windows rolled up," Darcy's mother said.

"I can't, Mom. I'll bake," Darcy pointed out.

"Well, stay in the truck, at least."

Her mother got out, slammed the door, and walked away quickly.

Darcy watched her mother until she couldn't see her anymore. Then she watched the sun throw vast shadows across the desert floor, turning the mesas the color of blood.

Darcy had to move. Her body was begging her to get out of the truck.

Slowly, carefully, she opened the door and eased herself out. Half crawling, half hopping, she made her way to a boulder just off the side of the road and sat down. She could feel the piece of pottery, still tucked in her shirt. And she started feeling the cold.

"At least it's a beautiful night," Darcy said, looking up at the sky.

The first planets were coming out. High overhead were Jupiter and, lower down and even brighter, Venus. Quickly they were joined by stars, more than she had ever seen. Darcy could name a few of the stars and constellations. One of her dreams was to own a telescope. Until they could afford one, she learned what she could about the story the sky spread out each night. The points of light comforted her now. She looked deep into the darkening twilight, seeking old friends—Orion, the Big Dipper.

She didn't hear the steps behind her until they were very close.

"You got trouble, little girl?"

The voice was deep.

Darcy turned, though it hurt to do so, and looked at the bent shadow beside the truck. It was an old man; she could see that much. A thin old man wearing a battered cowboy hat with a broken feather in it.

"You got trouble, little girl?" he said again.

It was stupid to be afraid of him. She'd just been startled.

"Yes," Darcy said cheerfully. "Car trouble."

"Tires look okay. Is it the engine?"

"I'm not sure. My mother's gone for help."

"Want me to take a look?" the old man said.

"Do you know about trucks?"

"Some. You got a flashlight?"

Darcy lifted herself to her feet and hobbled to the truck. She got the flashlight out of the glove compartment and handed it to the old man. She managed to reach across the seats and unlatch the hood.

The old man lifted the hood and peered beneath it.

"How come you out here all alone?" the old man said.

"It was weird," Darcy said. "We went out to visit the ruins at Chaco Canyon. I twisted my knee. We were on the way back to town when we hit a coyote. At least we thought we hit him, but when we got out to look, he wasn't there."

"Long way to town," the old man said, and slammed the hood down. "You got anything to eat?"

"Can you fix the truck?" Darcy said.

"Nope. You got anything to eat?"

There was a hint of menace in the way he asked.

"We had some bread and chocolate," Darcy said. "But I'm pretty sure the chocolate's melted and the bread's stale by now. They've been in the truck all day."

"Doesn't matter," the old man said.

Darcy gave him the food and he wolfed it down, shoving the bread into his mouth with both hands. It made her feel sorry for him.

"You must have been hungry," she said.

"Pretty much all the time," the old man said, and licked his fingers. "You got any men with you?"

"No," Darcy said. "Just me and my mother."

The old man shook his head.

"Bad to be out here all alone. Bad things happen sometimes."

"Women don't need men around all the time," Darcy said.

"Just when their trucks break down, maybe," the old man said.

The moon was up now, but it gave off little light. The old man's outline had disappeared. He was part of the night.

"Why did you come out here, anyway?" His voice came to her across the darkness. "Just to see old stones?"

Darcy wasn't going to tell him about her father, about the promise they were keeping. "We wanted to have an adventure," she said.

"Well, you're having one."

"Not the one we wanted, that's for sure."

"Old stones. Stupid to be here," the old man said.

"There's nothing stupid about it! Haven't you ever wanted to know about the Anasazi? The people who were here first?"

"Nope," the old man said. "Navajo say those are bad places. Full of evil spirits. Why didn't you stay away?"

"Because they're important, scientifically. And no one believes in evil spirits anymore."

The wind blew. The old man was silent. At last he said, "What do they believe in?"

"Science," Darcy said. "Progress."

"Good." The old man thumped the hood of the truck. "Real good."

"What do you believe in?" Darcy asked.

"Eating."

"Oh," Darcy said.

"What about you, little girl? What do you believe in?"

"As I said. Science and logic."

"You really believe in those things? Or do you just believe you believe in them?"

Was he playing with her? Why would he do that? "What do you mean?" Darcy asked. "I don't think I understand you."

"What someone believes is what they believe all the time," the old man said. "Not just what you believe when the sun's up and the truck's running good. When things go bad, when it gets dark, when you get lost. What do you tell yourself then? What do you believe right now?"

Suddenly, he was standing right next to Darcy, close enough that she could see his eyes, even in the dark. *They're yellow*, she thought. "Uh—what do you think the stars are?" she asked, trying to keep her voice from squeaking.

"Huh?" the old man said.

"I believe the stars are huge balls of hydrogen burning millions of light-years away from here," Darcy said, as brightly as she could. "I believe they're millions of years old. You can see so many stars here. The most I've ever seen. You must have some interesting ideas about them."

The old man seemed surprised. He took a step back.

"Who tells you this stuff?" he asked.

"Scientists. Astronomers."

"They ever go there and see 'em?"

"No," Darcy said. "Not yet."

"Maybe stars are campfires for ghosts. All the old ghosts up there. Sitting by fires that never warm them. Always hungry, maybe."

"Ever go there and see?" Darcy asked.

"Maybe," the old man said. "Maybe stars are just stars. But what do you believe about this place? Bad place. Place where maybe nobody wanted you to come. Pretty far out here. Pretty dark. No food. No men. No science. What do you believe right now?"

"I believe my mother will be back with help," Darcy said.

And, out of the night, far up the road, lights appeared. Many lights, yellow and white. The faint sound of a powerful engine approaching. Darcy knew it was a tow truck, coming fast.

The old man stepped back off the road. For a second, Darcy thought he had disappeared, but he had only moved away from her.

In two minutes, the truck was there. They were the longest minutes of her life.

It was a huge yellow machine with BEGAY TOWING AND SERVICE painted in blue on the side. The door opened and her mother jumped down, smiling.

"Don't worry, Darcy! The cavalry's here," she almost sang.

"Pardon me, ma'am, but around here we don't think too much of the cavalry. General Custer, you know." It was a young man who spoke with a smile. He looked as powerful as his truck. His eyes were bright.

Darcy's mother laughed. "Darcy, this is Chris Begay. He's going to save us."

"Going to try to, anyway," Chris said. "Let's take a look."

Then he saw the old man. "Ya-Ta-Hey, Grandfather," he said.

"Oh. Is this your grandfather?" her mother asked, surprised to see the old man.

"No. Just being respectful," Chris said.

"He just showed up a little while ago," Darcy said. "He's been keeping me company." Maybe if she said it that way, it would be true. She turned to the old man. "I'm sorry, I never asked your name."

"Billy, maybe," the old man said grudgingly.

"What clans, Grandfather?" Chris asked. "My mother was Red House, and my father is Turning Mountain. How about you?"

The old man didn't seem to like the truck's bright lights. "You know Hosteen Begay?" he asked.

"The one who lives over by Spider Rock?" Chris said. "He's my real grandfather."

"Uh-huh. Thought so, maybe."

"Well, a lot of people know my grandfather," Chris said. "He's kind of famous. Knows a lot about the old ways. He walks in beauty, that one."

The old man didn't answer.

"Where do you live, Grandfather?" Chris went on. "Not many of our people out this way."

"Got a little place up by the canyon," the old man said.

"Guess the old stories don't scare you, huh?" Chris asked.

"Too old to be scared of much," the old man said.

"But didn't you tell me bad things happen here?" Darcy blurted out. She hadn't meant to mention any of the creepy things he'd said to her.

"Bad things happen anywhere," the old man said.

"That's true," Chris said. "Here. In town. Any place you go. But the canyon's special. My grandfather taught me to be respectful."

"Respectful's good," the old man said.

"Well, let's take a look at that engine," Chris said. "Pop the hood." After checking it, he said, "Battery's low. Not dead, just not strong enough to turn your engine. Weird, but it happens. I'll get my cables and give you a jump."

But even when their truck was hooked up to the mighty tow truck, it didn't start.

"Mmm," Chris said. "Let's take another look." After a minute, he said, "Tell me, Grandfather. Did you try to help?"

"Just looked," the old man said.

"And when you looked, what did you see?"

"Nothing."

"Come on, Grandfather. Give it back," Chris said.

"Give what back?"

"The little piece you stole. The distributor rotor." He held out his hand.

"But he didn't take anything," Darcy said. "I was watching the whole time."

Chris ignored her, still holding out his hand. "Do what is right," he said.

"I'm not the only thief here!" the old man snarled.

"Give it up, Grandfather," Chris said. "This time you lose. I have you." With his other hand, Chris tore a small leather bag free from his own neck. The old man growled and cringed. He turned to run, but Darcy had limped to a place right behind him. As the old man bolted, he knocked her down, but she managed to hold tight to him. She felt the piece of pottery gouge her ribs as he scrabbled to be free. She felt her knee flame with pain. She heard her mother scream. Then there was an odd taste in her mouth, something dry and powdery, and the old man was gone.

A small piece of black plastic lay in the sand beside her. She handed it to Chris. Her mother helped her stand up. Darcy ran her tongue around her mouth. The taste of dust was strange, but good somehow.

"What was the stuff you sprinkled on the old man?" Darcy's mother asked.

Chris shrugged. "A little juniper dust."

"But why?" Darcy asked.

"Good for protection from evil," Chris went on. "Well, let's fix what ails your engine." He put back the distributor rotor.

When Darcy's mother tried the key, the engine came to life. "What a beautiful sound," she said. She left the engine running and got out of the car to pay Chris.

"But why did that old man steal the rotor?" Darcy asked Chris. "Why did he want to hurt us?"

Chris closed the hood of their car and carefully wound up the cables that ran between his battery and theirs. Then he said, "Promise to believe me?"

"Yes," Darcy said. "Tonight, I can believe anything."

"That coyote you hit today?" Chris said. "That was him."

"You mean he was a ghost?" Darcy asked.

"No. Bigger than a ghost. A spirit. Old Man Coyote. He goes back a long way. And he likes to cause trouble."

"How did you know it was him?" Darcy asked.

Chris shrugged again. "Your mama told me you hit a coyote. She stops the car. No coyote there. Then your car won't start, for no reason. Seemed logical."

"Scientific," Darcy agreed.

"He was just a nasty old man," her mother said. "When we get back to town, we're calling the police."

"Whatever," Chris said. "Follow me back to my place. Don't get too far behind."

"No problem," Darcy's mother said.

They got into their car and started slowly away, keeping close behind Chris's truck.

Darcy still had her prize. The potsherd was still whole. She could feel it.

I'm a little like Old Man Coyote myself, she realized. *I've stolen something, too.*

The pain settled into her knee as if finding a home there.

Darcy began thinking, *Maybe this beautiful shard isn't the perfect gift, after all. Maybe I should've left it where I found it, where it belongs.*

She looked back at the spot where she'd grappled with the old man. Standing in the middle of the road was a coyote as big as a wolf. It was watching her with yellow eyes.

THE COFFIN DELIVERIES

by Kevin Emerson

The first coffin arrived on the porch of 14 Simmons Street on Wednesday, October 26, at 3:25 P.M., the same day that the first of the neighborhood pets disappeared. Tyler knew because he was there, walking home with his next-door neighbor, Jamie.

The big brown delivery truck rumbled by as they left the school parking lot, but neither Tyler nor Jamie noticed. Tyler was too busy turning his feet sideways and dragging them along the sidewalk, scraping up big piles of brown oak leaves. The piles grew to his knees, then began to overflow around and between his legs. When he looked back, he saw two wavy tracks up the sidewalk, revealing the wet concrete beneath.

"Ugh, why do you have to *do* that?" Jamie groaned. Tyler looked over to see her brushing clingy leaves off of her school-uniform khaki pants. "I'm gonna have to wash these again!" she muttered. "And look at you!"

Tyler saw that his pants were speckled with mud and leaf bits, and he felt clammy wetness soaking through his socks, but he just replied, "I don't care."

"Whatever," said Jamie. "*I* would. Now, where was I?"

"The part about the no whining," Tyler reminded her.

"Oh, right . . ." Jamie reached up and continued weaving a braid that was falling down in front of her face. Whenever Jamie told a story, she braided her hair, saying that it helped her to remember all the details. Tyler liked hearing her stories, even though she was a girl, because in any story told by Jamie, you knew you were going to get all the juicy details, way more than anyone else could remember, and always told in the right order to make the story the most interesting it could be.

This was because Jamie took her detail gathering seriously. Whenever there was an exciting story, she would interview everyone around her in every class and fill the margins of her notebooks with all the details. Then, at lunch, she would use her special set of highlighting markers—the neon six-color set—to organize these details into groups. Tyler had seen her do this enough to know the categories: Yellow = *the beginning*. Orange = *the middle*. Hot Pink = *you think it's the end, but it's not*. Sky Blue = *the plot twist*. Lavender = *the real ending*. Magenta = *the backstory* (Jamie explained once that even though you usually tell the backstory first, you don't really know it until you've got all the other details, so you have to go back and add it).

Jamie had already told the story of the missing pet three times. Tyler knew this by the three long, perfect braids that she'd already finished and tied with teal elastics. She was currently braiding her fourth. The rest of her thick black hair was gathered in a headband.

"So," she continued, "you know how, like, Dawn and Naamah have that cream-colored cat, right?"

"They named it Dawgs," said Tyler, concentrating on his leaf trails. He'd already heard this part.

"Right. Well, last night when they went to bed, Dawgs was still out, which is no big deal, 'cause she always stays out and terrorizes the raccoons, but then this morning, no whining."

"At the back door," Tyler added. He was watching his feet, and frowned because they had just reached a clean stretch of sidewalk, the leaves all raked away, the concrete dry and boring. Ahead, he heard a squealing and then a dry scraping, but he was busy gazing up expectantly at Jamie, only a year older than him, but a whole foot taller.

"Right," said Jamie, braiding busily. "No whining at the back door. And Dawgs didn't show up even when Naamah put out a milk bowl, and that, like, never happens."

"She probably got hit by a car," said Tyler. Of course, he knew that wasn't the case, because Jamie would not be on her fourth braid if the story ended in such a boring way. He just said it to keep things moving.

"There's no way," said Jamie authoritatively. "I checked with every kid who walks to school. Jamal comes down Dot Ave. Nothing there. Denzel didn't see anything on Wainright, Christopher was on Dexter. . . . If Dawgs was roadkill, we'd know."

"Mmm," Tyler agreed.

"But here's the thing," said Jamie. "Danny heard from Carlos, who heard from Tanya, that Charlene's cousin David, you know, the guy with the motorcycle—"

"That guy who always goes back and forth outside school really loud during math?"

"That's him—and you *know* Charlene pays him to do that—well, he said that he heard Dawgs meowing in the street last night, but then she just stopped meowing, like something *got* her."

"Huh. What do you think—"

Suddenly, a sound exploded beside them.

KA-THUNK!

Tyler and Jamie both halted and turned to find a muscled, brown-suited delivery-truck driver staggering backward, wincing in pain and grabbing at his foot. A long cardboard box lay cockeyed against the back of the truck, a wheeled cart overturned beside it. The box was over six feet long, maybe three feet wide, and looked heavy. There were stamps all over it, with urgent-looking words in another language. The driver grabbed the cart off the ground and shoved its base beneath the box. Tyler saw him straining and puffing as he lumbered by them.

Jamie's voice shrank to little more than a whisper. "No way," she said.

"What?" asked Tyler.

"Duh," she huffed quietly. "Look."

Tyler followed her pointing finger. There was a thin black line on the otherwise spotless sidewalk. It wavered back and forth, like it was drawn in chalk by Tyler's younger sister, Kara. But this wasn't chalk. It was thicker, and the pile was higher. It looked like dirt.

Creeaak-THUNK!

The driver had begun lifting the box up the wooden steps of the house beside the clean sidewalk. Each time he raised it up a step, the box would roll back and slam against the next step, and a small cloud of black would puff out of the base of the box, through a torn hole in the cardboard. Something reflected, like shiny metal, through the hole.

Creeaak-THUNK!

"Come on!" Jamie grabbed him by the backpack strap and yanked him into the street. They raced between parked cars to the leaf-strewn safety of the far sidewalk, then ducked behind a station wagon and peered out.

The driver had reached the front door. Like its neighbors to either side, the house was three stories tall, with a porch on each floor. But this building hadn't been turned into three separate apartments, like the houses Tyler and Jamie lived in. It was occupied by a single resident. The paint was well kept, a dark bloodred, with black window trim. Heavy wooden blinds hung down behind each window. The blinds were shut, as they always seemed to be.

Tyler knew why: Mr. Karloffski was a vampire. Everybody knew that.

Or, at least, everybody *said* that, but it was like when everybody said that their classmate Carlos was from another planet. Mr. Karloffski couldn't *really* be a vampire—

The driver rang the doorbell. Tyler heard a deep tone, like a sad wind chime.

"This is unreal," said Jamie. She'd left her braid incomplete, a little broom of frizz still at its end.

"What?" asked Tyler, not because he didn't know, but because he wanted to make sure Jamie was thinking the same thing he was. . . .

"Duh!" she snapped. "That's obviously a coffin!"

Yup, they were thinking the same thing.

"And everybody knows that vampires sleep in coffins filled with their own soil, from their native lands," Jamie continued. "If Mr. Karloffski is having vampires shipped to his house"—Jamie was speeding up now like she could when she really got excited about a new story—"then maybe he's, like, building a vampire army, and they'll take over our neighborhood first and turn us all into bloodthirsty monsters and then we'll take over the city and then the country and then we'll join forces with Transylvania, 'cause that whole country is vampires, and then—" She stopped.

The door had clicked open. It swung inward into darkness. Like a rising moon, a white face appeared, thin with sagging cheeks, and deep shadows over the eyes from bushy eyebrows. Two white hands floated out of the dark and took the signing pad from the driver.

They heard the driver ask, "You want me to wheel it in?"

There was a mumbled response, and the door closed.

The driver shook his head and leaned the long coffin box against the wall. He hurried down the steps and back into his truck. It rumbled to life and lurched away up the street.

Tyler and Jamie stared at the box. It seemed eerily quiet on the street. Tyler wondered where all the birds had gone. Sure, many had flown south for the winter, but where were the chattering pigeons, the arguing crows?

"Let's go," said Jamie, and yanked Tyler along again.

Tyler didn't protest. As they hurried away, he forgot to make leaf trails. He was too focused on glancing back at the dirt-leaking, coffin-shaped box on the porch of the old vampire's house.

* * *

Before Tyler got to school the next morning and heard about the second pet disappearance, he shuffled out the door in his big black parka with his favorite football team's logo and felt a splash of freezing air against his face. His sneakers slipped on a thin layer of sparkling frost. The sun wasn't yet over the tall houses, but orange rays split the alleys between them and lit the street with tiger stripes. The whole scene made Tyler forget about coffins and vampires. He followed his usual route to school, making trails in the stiff, icy leaves.

Tyler was nearing the parking lot when he heard a horrible sound. A wailing. Sad and in pain. He stopped, only to find himself on clean concrete. Mr. Karloffski's dark house loomed over him. The coffin was gone from the porch.

He heard the sound again. It seemed to be coming from behind the house. A miserable whining, and it sounded a lot like a cat. Could it be Dawgs, desperate for food, dying from the cold, and Tyler his only hope for survival? He took a step—then something caught his eye, the blinds of a window upstairs, fluttering, like he was being watched. Tyler tore off toward school.

He found Jamie at lunch, surrounded by notebooks, her limp school hamburger untouched on a plastic tray nearby. Her highlighters were scattered about, tops off, ready.

"What?" she snapped. "There's a second pet missing. I have to re-highlight everything! So spit it out already."

Tyler did.

Jamie's brow furrowed. "Go away," she muttered, highlighters blazing.

* * *

When they left school that afternoon, Jamie was busily working on her sixth braid with neon-stained hands. "They have the backyard completely fenced in," she said as Tyler re-carved his leaf trails, "but Denzel's dog, Grover, was gone this morning."

"Maybe it jumped out," said Tyler, knowing it hadn't.

"Duh." Jamie rolled her eyes. "Pomeranians are, like, the littlest dogs in the universe. They can't jump higher than a kneecap. And—"

Tyler looked up to find her stopped in her tracks, staring ahead with wide eyes. He felt his sneaker soles scuff on clean, dry sidewalk, and he probably knew what he was going to see before he even turned. . . .

And he was right.

There, in the shadow of Mr. Karloffski's porch, a second long box leaned beside the door.

"Two coffins . . ." Jamie breathed. "Two pets. There's got to be a connection." Tyler could almost hear her highlighting in her mind.

On Friday, Charlene's pet gecko, Alfonzo, disappeared. That afternoon, the third coffin was delivered.

On Saturday, it was Omar's tetra fish, named Mr. Diabolical. And coffin number four.

Sunday. Neil and Carla's Labrador retriever, Noodles. And coffin number five.

Monday. Halloween. School was abuzz, but nobody knew of a sixth missing pet. Jamie even had Shawn call home because he couldn't quite remember where he'd last seen his ant farm, but then his dad found it. Also, Jamal and Nadina had both reported hearing miserable wailing sounds by Mr. Karloffski's house over the weekend. Jamal had even told his mom, but she had just said, "Whatever, that's crazy." It didn't help that each coffin was always off the porch by the time everybody's parents got home from work.

Tyler sat by Jamie at lunch, watching her re-highlighting again. Most of her notes were triple-colored by this point and had turned to gross shades of brown.

Tyler was dressed as a pirate. Jamie was a zombie, her face and arms painted with grays and greens. She'd splattered one of her mom's lab coats with red paint.

"The beginning of the story is still the first pet," Jamie muttered. "But no pet today."

"So that's the end?" asked Tyler hopefully.

Jamie looked at him like he'd given the wrong answer in math class again. "We don't know the backstory. Which means . . ." She picked up the hot-pink highlighter and wagged it at him. "*You think it's the end, but it's not.*"

Tyler didn't like the sound of that.

They left school in the gloomy afternoon. It had rained all morning, and a low fog remained over the city. The world was murky and slightly brown.

Jamie was busy braiding. She was down to her last clump of free hair. She'd added beads to the other braids, and with each step they clattered together. Because she was dressed like the risen dead, it sounded like bones.

"Halloween," said Tyler, just to kick Jamie out of her thoughtful silence. He carved fresh canyons in the leaves. "Where are you gonna go trick-or-treat—"

Jamie threw her arm in front of him. "He needs one more," she said quietly.

Tyler saw the clean concrete at his feet. And on Mr. Karloffski's porch: the sixth coffin.

Just then they heard a quiet whimper. Tyler turned and peered up the driveway. Something was moving. It was hard to make out in the fog, but it looked black and floppy.

Jamie took a hesitant step. "Noodles?" she called. The Labrador barked in return. Jamie's voice fell to a whisper: "Come on." She hurried up the driveway.

Tyler felt a great rush of worry. This was not good. But then Noodles barked again, and Tyler felt sure that he'd never heard a more desperate, please-get-me-out-of-here cry.

They passed a spilled mess of trash cans beside the house on their right. Black bags popped like enormous squished insects, blue recycling bins overflowing with bottles and cans, an old broken lamp atop it all. Mr. Karloffski's side had only three perfect steel cans, lids on tight.

Tyler caught up with Jamie as she was petting Noodles on the head. He was peering through an open gate in a tall wooden fence and straining against a thick rope around his neck. His pink, rubbery tongue slapped against Jamie's zombie-painted arm, leaving streaks.

"How'd you get here, boy?" Jamie asked.

Tyler's gaze wandered past the dog, into Mr. Karloffski's backyard. He wasn't sure what he was looking at, but then he heard another desperate sound. Scratching. Like claws against wood.

Jamie pushed the gate farther open. Its hinges creaked. They saw a perfectly manicured lawn—

Except for three square mounds of dirt. They looked like filled-in holes.

On the far side of the yard were two more dirt mounds, one large, one small, beside two holes in the ground. The large hole had a dog-size wooden crate beside it. And beside the small hole was a little wooden box. Something scratched desperately inside, making the box shake.

"The missing pets," Jamie whispered. She took a step back. "He's burying them alive—"

Tyler heard her bump against something soft. Noodles snarled, baring his fangs.

Don't turn around, Tyler thought. But he did.

A towering figure loomed over them, draped in a long black coat, collar upturned. The face was shaded by a wide hat. "Sleep," a thin voice hissed. A bone-white hand waved before them.

Tyler stumbled. The fog wrapped around him, washing out the world, erasing it to darkness. . . .

Tyler opened his eyes to find himself in a dim room. He was tied to a tall chair, seated at a long dining table with a burgundy tablecloth and silver plates and cutlery. A huge chandelier of candles hung above them like a great silver spider. Tyler struggled, but the ropes held tight.

"Tyler!" Jamie whispered. She was beside him, tied up as well. He met her terrified gaze. Outside, he heard a stinging sound, metal against stones, like a shovel.

"We have to get out of here!" Jamie cried.

"How?" Tyler wondered desperately. He looked around—

Then he saw the coffin lying directly behind the chair next to his. "Coffin!" he blurted out. It was made of dark, polished wood with silver trim. On top of it was a silver *K*.

"Here, too," Jamie said. Tyler looked behind her: another chair with another coffin beside it. "And over there." Jamie pointed with her chin. There were four more chairs around the table, a coffin behind each.

"And *those*," said Jamie. Tyler followed her gaze upward. Hanging down on chains, directly above five of the chairs, were shiny copper cages. They seemed to be empty. There were no cages above their own seats or above the chair at the head of the table.

"What are they for?" Tyler wondered, but Jamie only gasped. The metal scraping outside had ceased, replaced by a new sound.

CLOMP . . . CLOMP . . . CREEAAK!

"He's coming!" Jamie struggled in her chair, trying to move it.

"It is quite pointless," a raspy voice said from the doorway. It sounded like velvet being torn. "There is no escape."

Mr. Karloffski entered the room. He pulled off dark-stained work gloves, revealing bone-white hands. He swept off his fedora, slick silver hair beneath. He slipped off his long coat and smoothed his rumpled black suit. Then he sat in the chair at the head of the table.

"Welcome," he said, his plaster face stretched in a grin. His irises were lavender, his pupils white and twinkling like pearls. "You are my guests of honor."

"You're going to kill us. . . ." Jamie whispered.

Mr. Karloffski glanced over his shoulder, to the grandfather clock in the corner. "Almost time," he purred, his grin widening, and Tyler saw the long vampire points of his teeth.

"No!" Tyler shouted, straining at his ropes.

"It has to be you," Mr. Karloffski said reasonably. "If I had let you go after what you'd seen, you'd have ruined this night. Besides, I think you'll enhance the meal." He reached out and picked up a silver carafe. What he poured into the crystal wineglass before him was dark red, and yet too thick to be wine. . . .

"We won't tell anyone!" Tyler begged.

The clock chimed shrilly.

"You must understand," said Mr. Karloffski, "this night can only happen once. The permits alone for this kind of magic have taken me more than fifty years to procure from those Half-Light bureaucrats. Finally, tonight, all the celestial bodies are in alignment, and the demigods of Morosia have granted me access to the *forces*. The time has come."

"You really *are* a vampire," Jamie sputtered. "You—you want to suck our blood."

Mr. Karloffski chuckled. "Well, naturally. But that's not why you're here." He inhaled deeply, and suddenly his eyes ignited in brilliant white. "*Morchess . . .*" he hissed.

"Help!" Tyler shouted.

Whispers blew around the room on swirling winds. Tyler saw lights glowing and heard a horrible whining sound. He strained to look behind him. Out the back window, he saw ghostly pink streams of light emerging from the dirt mounds in the backyard, all crying out at once. They drifted toward the house. The back door slammed open. The pink streams flowed into the room, their howling deafening.

Each light entered one of the hanging cages and sharpened into the image of its buried animal. Tyler saw little glowing ghosts of Dawgs, Mr. Diabolical—even Noodles, whose ghost had shrunk to fit the cage. They all yelped and scratched wildly at the bars.

"*Rise . . . ,*" Mr. Karloffski commanded.

Now Tyler heard an even worse sound. The creaking of coffins yawning open . . . the ruffling of dirt falling from clothing, the shuffling of old arms and legs rising. Five figures stood, brushing off their soiled suits and dresses with decayed hands. Their faces were brown and skinless, but their eyes were still white, with glowing red pupils.

"Meet my family," Mr. Karloffski said proudly as they took their seats.

"They're not vampires," Jamie said hoarsely.

"Sadly, no," said Mr. Karloffski, and Tyler was surprised to hear a hitch in his voice. Tears slipped down the old man's white cheeks as he appraised the five risen corpses. "My mother, Katarina; my father, Reinhold; my sister, Claire; my brother, Emil; and my dear wife, Naomi."

"Dearest Berthold," said Naomi, her bony jaw clicking beneath a wedding veil. "How wonderful to see you again."

"Are these morsels for us?" snarled Reinhold, gazing at Tyler with his one remaining eye. Then he noticed Jamie in her zombie costume. "Ah, one of our own. A pleasure . . ."

"Settle down, Father. These are my neighbors," said Mr. Karloffski. "The girl is not one of us, and no, they're not on the menu. I thought they could entertain us with their knowledge of the modern age." He turned to Tyler and Jamie. "My family was executed during the Russian Revolution. I alone escaped."

"We have missed you so, Berthold," said Katarina.

"The backstory," Jamie breathed with relief. "But what about the sixth coffin?"

Mr. Karloffski kept gazing at his family. "That is for me. In order to have this dinner, I sold my inner *vampyr* spirit. When we are done this evening, I shall join my family in eternal slumber, and we will journey home. Ah, which reminds me . . ."

Mr. Karloffski rummaged in his pocket. He pulled out a small stack of square papers and placed them in front of Jamie. Tyler saw that they were shipping labels. "When we are finished, your ropes will unbind. Before you go, though, I hope you could do me two favors: Please affix one of these labels to each coffin. I have arranged for our pickup just before dawn. Second, perhaps you could gather your friends and dig up the pets in the backyard."

Jamie's face went pale.

"Relax, dear, they're alive," said Mr. Karloffski. "I just briefly borrowed their souls. Their energy was needed to raise the dead." He nodded to the cages. "Like batteries."

"What's a battery?" asked Emil, fingering the bullet holes in his jacket.

Mr. Karloffski sighed with an expression that Tyler understood: the annoyed older brother. "The children will explain later. Now, let us dine and dance until dawn!"

He stood and began filling goblets with the worrisome red fluid. But then, as the relatives slurped, Mr. Karloffski returned with much more normal dishes—roast duck and mashed potatoes. There was also something deep-fried, with many eyes, like rats, but Tyler ignored that.

The sky was brightening when Tyler and Jamie stumbled out of Mr. Karloffski's house. They had been tied up all night, but, as it turned out, the conversation had been fun, at least compared to being eaten. They had even dozed off as the family danced to old records in the living room.

Sure enough, as dawn approached, the Karloffskis had hugged and then taken their places back in their coffins. With another hissed command, Mr. Karloffski released the animal souls to the yard. He closed the lids on his relatives and paused, standing over his own coffin. He sighed. "Thank you," he told Tyler and Jamie. "If you could just wait until we've been picked up before you get found, I would so appreciate it."

Jamie nodded. "Okay. So, but . . . that's it? You did all this just for last night?"

"It was enough," the old vampire said quietly. He stepped into his coffin and closed the lid.

Tyler and Jamie watched from the side of the house as two deliverymen struggled with the last boxed coffin. Once the truck was rumbling up the street, Tyler and Jamie walked out into the road. Police lights fell on them. There were screams, and shouts of joy, and the arms of relieved parents.

"This is the real end, right?" Tyler said to Jamie.

Jamie nodded, busily undoing all of her braids so she'd be ready for school.

WHERE WOLVES NEVER WANDER

by Joshua Gee

"Silence, wolves! Rest your paws on that granite perch. It is time to tell you why our kind of wolf must never journey farther than this—the lowest cliff on Wolfsbane Mountain."

Old Gretchen's head hung low while she paced back and forth, the ground crunching beneath her four paws.

Everything is different about the outside world, she thought as she crouched wearily. *Even the gravel sounds strange.*

Her seven young traveling companions knew that she was uneasy. Her left, graying ear—her "good" ear—was twitching up and down, again and again. She was monitoring for danger.

The pups jostled for the perfect spot. But the rocks were sharp and jagged here, unlike the smooth, sparkling surfaces of the inner caverns where mountain wolves lived.

"Be comfortable," said Old Gretchen. "But not too comfortable! The moon is drifting close to the peak, and the caverns call for our return."

It was true. There, at the great, yawning mouth of their cave, the wind made an eerie noise that delighted the seven pups.

"Oooooh-oooh," mimicked the small dark pup named Fangdon. All of them began howling delicately in unison, struggling to find the right pitch.

"HUSH!" barked Old Gretchen. "Or they will hear you!"

The pups went silent again.

"Silly superstitions," growled young Krowler under his breath. "Everybody knows there's no such thing as humans."

Of all the Ranger Scouts, Krowler was always the quickest with a mean remark. But this time, the other pups were quick to quiet him, clawing gently at his face.

If Old Gretchen heard him, she didn't show it.

"Tonight, and only tonight, I will tell you the truth about where the day can take you. Because each of you is old enough to know." She glared at one of the pups with her ancient yellow eyes. "Even you, little Krowler . . ."

"I knew it," whispered one of the pups. "She's going to tell us the story about the humans."

"I told you tonight was the night!" shouted another pup, whose nose was dripping from the chill of the late autumn air.

"Oh, you expect *humans*, do you? Well . . . perhaps. But first I will tell you about my brother."

"The one who disappeared?" asked Krowler. Even he was paying attention now.

Old Gretchen nodded.

"Did he . . . die?"

"No, Krowler. Worse than that."

"What could be worse than death?"

Before the pups knew it, Old Gretchen's story had begun.

It was during the time of the Great Famine—when the elk and the fox no longer roamed our Feeding Fields at night. But before the Elders lured the precious herds of goats that sustain us now.

Young or old, we hungered alike. Young or old, every mountain wolf shared the same pain when we laid our heads to sleep every morning. So it seemed to me as though we also shared one mission: *Find food.*

And I knew exactly where I was going to find it.

My mission had already led me to the edge of the humans' world at a cliff called Double-Fang Door. Before departing down the mountain, I was performing calculations in the dirt with my claw.

"Why can't *I* be Navigator?" asked my brother, Argus.

I was trying to ignore him. "The moon is three cliffs past the peak right now," I said, thinking aloud while I drew a triangle beneath a circle and a square, "and the place I want to go is two paws beneath the valley. . . ."

Argus, meanwhile, was leaping up and down, trying to capture my attention. "Don't forget to draw the humans!"

Argus had been taught—as you all have—that humans are just a superstition. But I knew better, even back then. I had been told things by an old wolf—he's long dead now. His name was Old Screecher, and everyone thought he was crazy. He told me all kinds of things about humans—where they lived, how they lived. I knew the names of many things that belonged to humans. But I never saw the objects to connect to the words. I hadn't observed a human in its natural habitat—or anywhere else for that matter. Perhaps in my nightmares, certainly not in real life.

Argus looked up at me with yellow eyes, his tail wagging in every direction.

"Okay, I'll draw *one* human for you," I said, sketching a crooked stick figure. "But I'm going to have to send you back home to the caves if you keep howling like this. Somebody will hear us."

"Somebody . . . or some*thing*," whispered Argus, staring at my drawing. With great care, he smoothed over one of the circles and added another line. "You got it backward," he said confidently. "Humans have two heads. But only one tail . . ."

He must've been listening to some of the older pups, who always claimed to know everything.

"Gretchen," he said, "what happens if we encounter one of the Elders on the way down? Won't they be coming back from the Feeding Fields?"

"Every night, the Elders return with their stomachs empty and their spirits broken. They're just as hungry as we are. So I think we should tell them the truth."

"The truth?"

"We tell them we're hunting for humans," I said as I sharpened my claws against the granite.

By the time we made our way down the mountain, the moon was already two cliffs past the peak. At least, that was my best guess.

I kept stealing glances at the twinkling stars above, anxiously performing calculations in my head, then performing them again and again.

"Humans mostly come out in daylight," Argus said. "Don't they?"

"Yes," I said. "Mostly."

"But they come out at nighttime, too, right? So we'll catch one?" His voice wavered.

"My plan might not be perfect, but we've got to try. The odds of locating a human at night may be low, but the odds of surviving daylight are . . . unknown." Old Screecher had told me many things, but not about that.

Argus got excited. "I heard that sunlight will curl your fur and turn it purple!"

Just then, I stumbled over what I thought was a rock, and tumbled, tailfirst, into some thistle bushes.

Argus instantly bared his fangs and attacked the strange black- and-white thing. . . . It popped! Argus squeezed the air out of the stretchy remnants.

"They call that a ball," I said. I knew the word. Now I had the object for it. "I'll explain later," I added.

Argus was fascinated.

As I flipped back to my feet, I scanned the horizon for the moon but saw only mountain. Its peak was far above us now. Too far.

That's when I realized the ball was only the beginning.

"Argus! Look! That big structure—it's a house! Houses mean humans. Now, if we could just figure out how much time we have left . . ."

"Don't worry! The moon's right over there!"

"Where? Wait!"

He had already sped off. "Maybe we can find some juicy salamanders on the way!" he called.

Argus led me in the direction of a stream trickling in the distance. I hadn't even heard it at first. He truly had the makings of a great Navigator.

"Nice work," I said as the soft, cool grass squished beneath my paws. "We'll walk in the water. That way, we won't leave a scent."

"Who are we hiding from?" asked Argus. "We're wolves, not goats. This mountain is ours."

"This mountain is no one's. And besides—"

"And besides?" he muttered, devouring a gooey green salamander he had just found in the water.

By then, I was staring at a pile of mud and gravel that stretched across the stream. "And besides," I said in a more serious tone, "we're not on Wolfsbane Mountain anymore."

He crouched alongside me and looked where I was looking. "What is it?"

"See those jagged crevices? There? In the mud?"

"Snake tracks?" Argus said.

"No snake is that big," I said. "Those are from wheels."

"Wheels?"

"They're round," I said. "They move things around, from place to place."

"You mean those tracks are human-made?"

"Or *machine*-made, I suppose."

I tried to imagine the size of the cars and trucks that could leave such deep imprints. Wolves, of course, don't need wheels. No animal does.

How must it feel to rely on machines to get from one place to another? I wondered. *No running. No pouncing. No secret summertime missions in the moonlight.*

"Humans are practically defenseless," I said, scanning the sky for the moon. "I wonder if it's time to head back. . . ."

"Don't worry! You're not the Navigator. I am." He leaped atop a log and pointed his nose just beyond the stream. "See—the moon is right over there, behind those trees."

I saw a flat, winding road and little else until . . .

A small bright light.

"Over there!" he said, frustrated. Then he darted off.

"Argus! Wait!"

We made it to the edge of the road, but no farther. Argus stopped in his tracks, and I slammed into him from behind, sending both of us tumbling into a ditch.

"That's not the moon," he said.

"I think you're right."

Cautiously poking my head up to get a look, I saw that the light was attached to something. "Wheels," I said.

"Like what made those tracks, before?"

"No, those came from a truck. I can see only two wheels, and trucks have more than that. This is called a bicycle."

"Gretchen! There's a human on it!"

The bright white light was nearly blinding to the eyes of a mountain wolf. Still, I could just barely make out two arms, two legs, and one head—plus a big cloth bag.

The human pulled something out of the bag and threw it right at us.

THWACK!

It just missed us by a tail's length as the bicycle whizzed past.

Argus sniffed at the object and discovered it to be a small bundle of paper, folded and rolled up, with human language printed all over it. Terrified, he bared his fangs and pulled back.

"It's okay," I said. "It's a newspaper. Come back over here in the bushes."

I gave him a moment to cool down. That's when I noticed the house again. The back entrance was just a few leaps away.

Houses mean humans, I reminded myself. *It's now or never.*

Argus was still staring at the small human riding away on the bicycle. My little brother's ears seemed to droop sadly while he waited to follow my lead.

"There wasn't much meat on its bones, was there?" I finally said. "Not much of a meal."

"No," Argus agreed. "What if we didn't eat him? What if we kept him in the cave with us? Like, as a pet?"

"Who's going to care for it, Argus? I'm not going to be the one who gets stuck with the chores. All the grooming and the feeding."

"But I feel sorry for him. He looked so helpless. So . . ."

"Furless," I whispered.

"Yeah, that."

"Argus, I *still* don't see the moon anywhere. Maybe we should head back now."

He squinted and stared at the sky. "Okay," he finally said. I think he was relieved.

It almost ended that easily.

Almost, but not quite.

One moment, it was just me and him. The next, it was me and him and something gigantic.

I remember only fragments of light and noise.

Our shadows suddenly flickering in front of us on the pavement . . .

A loud, mechanical crunching noise from behind us . . .

A truck SCREEEEEEECHed to a halt as it drove above us. We scrambled out from under it. . . .

A mountain wolf's fur can protect it from anything, I thought as I tumbled into the bushes. *But surely not this.*

A loud *BOOM!*

And then . . . silence.

Did I spot a flash of fur across the road?

"Argus!" I shouted. "Argus!"

No response.

"Where are you, you stupid wolf?" I cried.

"Gretchen!"

He was okay. With a sigh of relief, I poked my head up just high enough to scan the horizon. I quickly saw that I was on the same side of the street as the mountain. Just a few moments earlier, it had been too dark to see anything that far away.

Sunrise, I thought.

If I turned tail right there, I could make it back. . . .

No. Not without Argus.

"I'm over here!" I barked as loudly as I could. "Quick! They can hear us!"

"I can't! They'll see me! I can't!"

Without thinking—for if I did, I might not have acted—I sprinted across the street toward him.

There were humans everywhere now, their tiny eyes gawking at my every movement. It seemed to last forever.

Vividly, I remember the hot friction on the pads of my feet, the clicking of my claws against the pavement, until finally I leaped into a dark ditch, and my brother followed.

"Over there," he whispered. "A cave."

He was gesturing toward a circular stone formation about twenty paces away.

It didn't look like a cave to me, but we had little choice. The sky was turning pale—a sickly shade of light blue.

By the time we zipped through the bushes, the moon was surely zero cliffs past the mountain. In fact, only the faintest outline of the moon remained.

It wasn't a cave—it was a well. Frantic, we squeezed our bodies down into it, and our thick, youthful fur protected us from the landing. The damp and cavernous place was filled with spiders, mud puddles, and tiny slimy pebbles. There was an underground stream down there, too—a means of escape.

"We'll be safe here," I whispered. "Only a mountain wolf's eyes can see in darkness like this."

"It almost feels like home!" Argus said, and howled.

That was a dangerous mistake. The sound echoed off the cold stone interior. It must have seemed even louder from the outside.

"Down there!" a human shouted from above. I understood the words, the human words, as if some long-buried part of me had known them all along.

The humans were gathering all around. Could they see us? No, it was still too dark. Or so I thought . . .

I slowly backed up, away from their line of sight, and into a crevice.

More than a crevice, I instantly realized. *A tunnel!*

I turned to beckon Argus, but he seemed transfixed by the sights above.

How many humans were there? As the group peeked down into the darkness of the well, their shadows loomed large on the cramped walls around us. . . .

Wait, I thought. *Shadows? Shadows mean sunlight!*

The rising sun was slowly illuminating the well.

"Gretchen! Look! It's beautiful."

One of the shadows pulled away. Then another.

"No . . . Argus . . ."

Transfixed by the strange beams of light that flickered and danced in the air, he closed his eyes, lifted his nose toward the sky, and tried in vain to sniff at the brightness.

"Ouch! It tingles! Gretchen . . ."

"Over here! It's safe in the shadows."

"Gretchen!"

He opened his eyes, but couldn't move. He only stared, forlornly, at the peculiar numbness in his paws. Like a baby pup that hadn't yet taken its first steps, he stumbled and fell to the ground. He couldn't seem to move his limbs, not even a single pace.

All the while, tiny glowing embers filled the air. Puffy clouds of smoke irritated my eyes. Then I noticed the air was filled with something else. Wisps of fur!

"Argus! Your fur! It's burning!"

For better or worse, it didn't last long. The fur burned away from his face, his neck, his arms. It was like watching a burning tree that was losing its bark.

"No! Gretchen! What's happening?"

"Quick! Get out of the sunlight!"

He let out a fierce howl, but only at first. On the next breath, his entire snout seemed to retract inward—like a sinkhole in the mud.

"It burns!" he screamed, in a voice that sounded low and eerie and not at all wolflike.

"What's going on?" shouted one of the humans.

"How did a boy get down there?" asked another.

I pounced toward Argus at full speed, but didn't make it far. As soon as my right paw touched the sunlight, I could feel my very bones begin to morph into something else—something un-wolflike. My skin felt as if it had been wrapped too tightly around my body.

I recoiled in horror as the fur on my front leg disintegrated into smoky orange cinders. With every passing moment, my leg no longer looked like a leg; it looked like an arm. A *human* arm.

Oblivious to pain, I again reached for my brother, but now I couldn't even see him.

"Argus!" shouted an unfamiliar voice.

No, I thought. *That's my own voice! A human voice . . .*

I was blinded by light and ash and fur. My right ear felt like it was on fire. I dove into the stream, to try to cool my face, and got pulled under. Even after my head emerged from the water, I could hardly breathe. Had I been choking on sunlight? No, my lungs were smaller!

I struggled to regain strength and finally skirted my way onto a secure ledge alongside the water. I knew that I was going to be okay now that I had escaped those awful rays of light. My leg was covered in fur again, but my ear . . . I would never hear out of that ear again.

But what about Argus?

A brightness radiated from around the corner of the ledge.

I slowly inched my way toward it, one paw in front of the other.

From the safety of the shadows, I squinted. Despite the itching and the tingling, I could make out two figures—a tall human and a smaller one. The tall one had descended a rope. He was wrapping the other in a blanket.

The small one didn't seem to mind.

"What's your name?" asked the tall one.

"Argus," said the other.

"Don't fret, Argus. We will save you from the wolf."

They both ascended into the sunlight.

"I waited all day for my brother to return," said Old Gretchen. "And then I waited most of the night. Eventually, hunger compelled me to find my way back to the caves of Wolfsbane Mountain."

"Did you ever see Argus again?" asked Krowler.

"No, never. But one night, I was sitting upon this cliff—the last remaining exit from the mountain. As I stared out into the moonlight, I was certain I could hear him howling in the distance."

"What did he say?"

"Words of caution. Mysterious words. Spoken in the melody of the mountain wolf, but somehow in a different tongue."

Old Gretchen quietly extended a claw, pushed some gravel aside, and sketched some tall lines in the dirt, followed by a circle for a head, but no tail.

"*Mistake me not for one of you,*'" he howled. "*For I am half of you, yet none of you.*'"

"The sickness of the sun," Krowler said.

"It's a sickness that lurks in all of us. Every mountain wolf, young and old. Certainly, those flickering rays of light will change you forever. To survive in daylight, with neither fur nor fangs, is within your grasp, but such madness is a fate I would not wish upon any of you. So come with me now, turn your tails to the horizon, and may you never see the light of day."

I, BLOODER:

BEING AN ANNOTATED ACCOUNT OF GRUESOME DEATH AND EXCEEDING GORE AMONG THE UNDEAD OF CENTRAL PARK

by Peter Lerangis

Even in the moonlight, I could read the headline in *The New York Times*:

HEIRESS MISSING
LAST SEEN WITH BOYFRIEND ON EAST SIDE

I stuffed the printout back into my pocket. I knew Grigsby was involved but I didn't know how. In Corrective Bloodletting class, she'd whispered, "*Meet me in the Ramble*," and then slipped me the article. That's all I knew.

I was shaking. Grigs could be impulsive. She had gotten into trouble for this very thing before. I hoped she hadn't done anything stupid.

The moon had dropped behind a grove of trees, so I couldn't see much, but I could hear the waterfall to our left. Straight ahead and up the hill, the spires of Belvedere Castle reached to the black sky. In an hour or so, the sun would be rising. *Where is she?* I glanced around frantically and ran into a tree.

Whomp.

"Yeeow!" I cried.

"Klutz," called my best friend, Maxillus, over his shoulder.

Max, like Grigsby, like everybody else I've ever known, is normal. They can see in the dark, cast death-light, and flit—that thing where you're not really walking, not flying, just kind of skimming silently over the ground.

"I can't flit," I replied. "And I don't have—"

"Night vision. I know." He turned around and glared a stream of bluish light at me. He knows I hate that. "Are you through with your excuses now, Ferrous? Just because you're differently abled doesn't mean you can't *try harder.*"

One thing about Max—he's honest. A jerk, but honest. He may hate me, but he talks to me. And he agrees to transubstantiate[1] through the granite with me. I need help doing that. Most of the others wouldn't stoop to doing that for me. They look at me with pity or pretend I'm like them. The Undead can be really hypocritical.

Let me tell you, it isn't easy being a Blooder.

My parents knew I was a mutant the moment I was born. Unlike the other cute babies in the incubator, I didn't chitter and I wasn't all shriveled and leathery. The nurses were horrified at my . . . *pinkness.* When I was a kid, I wore fake fangs, stayed out of the sun, developed a taste for dried moth wings and household pets, and even wore pale makeup. Mom and Dad were worried about my mental stability.

1 *Eng.*: To change into another object; *Vamp.*: To modify body structure in order to travel through a solid object and emerge unchanged.

They joined Vamp-Anon, hoping to share their misery, but no one else had a genetic freak[2] for a kid.

Every Christmas, they'd ask me if I'd like to be bitten and killed. But many years ago the Zero-Growth Population Council Edict made human biting illegal. They say the Crypt in the Rock is over 100 percent occupancy, immortality means very little turnover, etc., etc. The thing is, I'm not technically human, and I wouldn't *add* to the population. But the Council always bogs down over ethics. They say there's almost no historical record for someone like me.[3]

And trust me, there are some fanatics about this overcrowding issue. Some of them, like this group called Martyrs of Homo Sapiens, say they *want* to go from vampire to human. To leave our society. That way, they can die. To ease the overcrowding. They want to do the opposite of what I want to do. They call the process *derevenation*.[4] Can you believe it?

There are two problems.

One. The process doesn't exist.

---

2 One out of 4,000 vampires carry the Blooder gene, but carriers appear totally normal. This is because the Blooder gene is *recessive*, which is a complicated way of saying (a) you can only be a Blooder if *both* parents carry the gene, but (b) even if they do both carry it, your chances of *being* a Blooder are still only 1 in 4. So, for you math geeks out there . . . in vampire society, the chance of two carriers marrying is $(1/4,000)^2$, or 1/16,000,000 (1 in 16 million). Thus, the chance of any offspring becoming a Blooder would be $(1/4) \times (1/16,000,000)$ or 1/64,000,000. That's 1 in *64 million*. Like I said, a FREAK!

3 The last sighting of a Blooder was in 1643, which no one remembers—except old Increase Flinders, who vaguely recalls feasting on "the poor unfortunate soul." It's known that he suffered mad indigestion (he still complains about it), but the whereabouts of said Blooder are unknown.

4 *De-* for "the opposite of" and *-revenation* for "the state of being a revenant." In the 21st century, we use the word *revenant* (which comes from the French, is fancy-sounding, and means "one who has returned from the dead") instead of *vampire*, which has become politically incorrect and will get you an icy blue death-glare if you use it.

Two. They're liars. *Who would not want to be normal and undead forever?*

I know. Wackos.

Anyway, I hear the whispers in school—"pinkie," "nice neck," "how's yer pulse?"— stupid stuff like that. Sometimes Max starts it. Honestly, the only time I ever feel free is after sunrise, when I'm the only one alive. Okay, I'm stuck in a vast, overcrowded underground crypt, but I get to read books and imagine things. It gets me so ramped up with excitement I can't even sleep.

"MWOOO-AH-HA-HA!" Max bellowed into the darkness, and I could hear the screams of two teenagers he'd caught alone on a park bench. He cackled hysterically as their footsteps receded toward the West Side. "God, I love doing that," he said as I approached.

"Um, isn't that a clear violation of the NYRC?"[5] I said.

Max rolled his eyes, casting blue light in a circle. "You are so . . . bloodless."

"What if those teens had garlic?" I chided. "Or a cross, or a wooden stake?"

"Then I'd discorporate[6] and decrease the surplus population, and the Council would rejoice." Max turned and began flitting to the crypt. "Lighten up, dude. It's been a long night. I just wanted a little release before D&D."[7]

As I entered the small meadow near the crypt, I felt a hand touch my shoulder from behind. A silken voice whispered, "Wait."

---

5 New Young-Revenant Code.

6 *Discorporation* (n.): Any process by which the body's molecules rearrange themselves in a symmetrical way, preparing to dehydrate and then become ash dust, either by the methods described above or by the action of the sun (see footnote 11).

7 Dehydration and Death.

Startled, I spun around. Grigsby was sucking nervously from a tube attached to a vacuum pack on her belt. "Want some?" she asked.

"I h-h-hate synthetic blood," I replied. Grigsby is the only person who makes me stutter. She has the most luminous eyes. Some people are put off by her directness, but I don't mind it at all.

"Not a vegan, eh? I have some real wolf blood, fresh-frozen from Alaska—expensive, helicopter-caught, top quality on the black market?" She cringed. "Sorry. I forgot you're a—"

"Freak?" I smiled. "N-never mind. Max is expecting me. He has to get me through the rock. Are you going to tell me why we're h-here?"

In reply, she glanced sadly at the moon for a moment, absorbing its light into her eyes, which allowed her to beam a weak photon stream across the meadow. It lit up a sign taped to a catalpa tree, a plea for help from a Roswell and Imogene Elkhorn in finding their beloved daughter Sundance. In the poster's center was an image of a smiling blond girl with small eyes, wearing what looked like a jeweled tiara and holding a tiny white poodle with a matching tiara.

"The heiress's name is *Sundance*?" I said.

"Was," Grigsby said.

"What did you do to her?" I demanded. Grigsby had been forced to do a year of community service in the synthetic blood lab after attempting to bite a wealthy teenage human, who managed to jam a BlackBerry into Grigs's mouth and chip a fang.

"Nothing!" Grigsby snapped. "But they're going to accuse me, I know it. And a second infraction can result in banishment—to the crypt below the Fresh Kills Landfill."

I felt for her. Fresh Kills was as good a place as any to be dead, but you could never get the smell out of your clothes the next night. We watched quietly as Max's silhouette flitted toward the base of the castle rock. Belvedere Castle is a tourist favorite in New York, a miniature stone fortress filled with nature exhibits and weather info, standing atop a huge granite outcropping with panoramic views of a great lawn.[8] In reality it's something much more—a gateway to a network of Undead that stretches for miles.

Near the point of entry, below a humming electrical substation, Max met a few other gathering revs. (I could hear the voices of Philomena Whitworth, Adriaen Van Blut, and Twig Bentley.) It looked like Philomena was whispering something into Max's ear. I could hear him laugh, and together they approached the rock, transubstantiated, and disappeared into the crypt, followed by the others.

"Guess he's not really expecting you, after all," Grigsby said.

I shrugged. "He probably forgot. He's a busy guy."

Grigsby turned suddenly. "Duck!" she cried out.

A shadow loomed toward me out of the dark sky. In the dim light, I could make out talons looming nearer.

"AAAAH!" I crumpled to the ground.

A huge hawk dropped past my head, its feathers all mangy and ruffled.

Thwaaack! It smashed against the castle rock, like it was drunk, and splatted onto the ground.

Grigsby let out a chitter of laughter—kind of a *fnif-fnif-fnif.*

"Not funny," I said.

---

8 Known as the Great Lawn.

"Sorry," she said. "I'm not laughing at you. That is one weird bird."

It's hard to stay mad at Grigs. She has the goofiest smile, and her skin is so translucent it seems to give off its own weak light. This is a really nice quality of born revenants.[9] (Crossovers[10] like Max, on the other hand, have to work at it.)

The hawk was now attacking an empty bottle, stabbing it angrily, trying to trap it in its talons and fly away, but stumbling back to the ground as its prey slipped out. Now, I see red-tailed hawks in Central Park all the time—but they never act like *this*.

Grigsby grabbed my hand. "Come with me. Sunrise is in thirty minutes. We have to do this before I mort."[11]

The Ichor Institute ("All Natural, All Organic, Tastes Like Straight from the Vein!") was not the first revenant company to develop synthetic blood, but theirs was the tastiest, and they drove the others out of business. Over the years, their enterprise grew from a small family-run interschistal[12] research laboratory to a vast factory and fulfillment center that encompasses the entire footprint of land under the Metropolitan Museum of Art (and soon to expand under the reservoir, pending a water-rights dispute).

Grigsby looked at the moon as she took my hand near the Egyptian wing. "Twenty-five minutes," she murmured. "Hang tight, dude."

---

9 One who is born of two revenant parents—which, technically, I am, too, or would be if not for my mutant freak condition.

10 Humans who become revenants by virtue of being bitten and killed by a revenant.

11 *Mort* (sl.): "To turn to dust by action of the sun." After Mordechai Yachad (d. 1847), a vampire who stayed in the sun too long and discorporated tragically at age 217.

12 *Interschistal*: "Embedded within granite."

Closing her eyes, she murmured, "*Salada dichtu moriere datu-nimachtano!*"[13]

"YEEEAAAAAGGHHHHHH!" You'd think I'd get used to melding into rock, considering I've had to do it *every night of my life*. My mom and dad have always assured me that I'll be able to do it by myself someday, without holding on to a revenant, and without the pain. But I don't believe them. It really, really hurts. Every time.

A moment later I was catching my breath, safely underground. As my vision cleared, I stared into the vast network of hallways, their stone walls aglow with gray-green mosslight. The light sconces were decorated with the Ichor symbol, twisting letters *I* that resemble two snakes. "Sorry about that," Grigsby said. "I forget how hard that is for you."

"I'm used to it," I lied.

"Be quiet," she said. "No one must know we're here."

I followed her as she walked on a twisty path through the lab. I was feeling creepy. The halls were empty, but you never knew if someone was working late. "So . . . the heiress was *here*?"

Grigsby stopped in front of a door marked AUTHORIZED REVENANTEL ONLY and gave me a grim glance. "I have to know I can trust you, Ferrous. You have to promise you will believe what I'm telling you."

I nodded. Grigsby had never lied to me.

She made a few complicated gestures with her fingers and muttered something that sounded like *Ramalachani al chthulula-gochni!*,[14] and the door instantly creaked open.

13 Basically something like "Open sesame" in Old Vampiric.
14 Which means "Please pass the hog intestines" in Old Vampiric. The truth is, I don't know exactly what she murmured, but I used this because it's one of the only other O.V. phrases I know.

The first thing I saw was a long table set against the far wall. On it were neat plastic cartons labeled with numbers. I walked closer and glanced inside.

My jaw fell open. In one of the cartons I saw a backpack, a mud-encrusted pair of sneakers, a hacky sack, and a cell phone. In another, there was a neatly folded pin-striped men's suit, some scuffed brown wingtip shoes, and a briefcase. I turned away. I didn't want to see any more. "Are they . . . dead?"

"Look in the last one," Grigsby said.

The container farthest to the left had a designer shirt and jeans, a black Tumi backpack—and a tiara placed on top.

"Sundance . . . ?"

Grigsby looked away.

I felt a little queasy. "But why . . . and why *here*? This is a company that makes artificial blood."

But Grigs was already muttering another incantation over another door, just to the right of the table.

As the door slid open, an acrid smell burst out of the room, overwhelming me, making my eyes water.

"Yuck, close it!" I cried.

But Grigsby was inside, and curiosity got the better of me. Holding my breath, I followed her. This room was pitch-dark, but Grigsby must have captured a lot of mosslight while I wasn't noticing, because her eye power was suddenly all over the place.

Cages lined the left wall, and they were filled with the foulest assortment of animals I'd ever seen—a jackal with a skunk-colored coat; an owl the size of a cougar, so big it couldn't move; a raven with the face of a lizard and a voice like a machine-gun rattle. All of them had something in common—sharp, accusing, murderous eyes that seemed to dig right under my skin.

I couldn't look. "What *are* they?" I asked.

"An experiment gone wrong—what else?"

A sign taped to the side of one cage read:

DO NOT FEED. DO NOT KILL.
DO NOT ALLOW CONTACT WITH BLOOD BEARER OR REVENANT.
BITE WILL IMMEDIATELY CAUSE CONVERSION OF PREY INTO PREDATOR OF INDETERMINATE GENETIC COMPOSITION.

"Grigs," I called out, "have you seen this—?"

But Grigsby was walking to the opposite wall, which was stacked with what looked like file cabinets.

As I got closer, I realized they were too big to be what I thought they were. She pulled one open, and I spotted a bone-white set of feet before I turned away in disgust.

"Harold Finster," she said. "February seventh of this year. Rachel Czolky, January twenty-first. Sammy Lonsdale . . ."

I had heard enough. I ran out the door and into the hallway. I have studied my Vampiric History, and I know horrible, shameful things have happened. But I've never seen anything like this. Our people are nonviolent. I can't stand involuntary death and gore. I was raised that way. Why was Grigsby showing me this? *How was she involved?*

Grigsby may have been calling after me, but I couldn't hear for the pounding of the blood in my head—which was, of course, something even Grigsby wouldn't understand.

All I could think was that I had given her so much slack. When others dissed her, called her a sneak and a biter, I'd stuck up for her. But she'd brought me here to show me bodies. To brag about her achievements. To teach me how to be a *real* revenant, not a squeamish, blood-bearing wimp.

I had never seen this side of Grigsby.

I had to get away. I couldn't trust her.

So I ran.

"Hey, where are you going?" she shouted. "Not *that* way!"

The corridor had no sharp corners, no lefts or rights, just swirling curves growing out of swirling curves, walls lined with closed doors. I followed them blindly. I could hear her behind me as I ran into a dead end.

I slammed my shoulder into the last door I saw. A door with a big *X* on it. Someone must have forgotten to lock it, because it gave way and I staggered inside.

I shut the door behind me. Spinning around, I ran smack into the last thing I would expect to find.

Me.

I must have blacked out, because I was on the ground when my eyes opened, and Grigsby was bent over me, looking concerned.

"Tell me it was a dream," I said.

"Why did you come here?" Grigsby was saying, her voice plaintive and anxious. "Why *here*?"

I looked up. Sure enough, there was . . . *me*. Grinning stupidly, standing frozen in position, about to shake someone's hand.

"It's not real," Grigsby grumbled.

I nodded. I could tell that. It was a hologram of me, standing in a column of light near a complicated control board. "What is it?" I asked.

Grigsby tried to pull me back to the hallway. "Never mind. You're not supposed to be here. We don't have time for this—"

I pulled back. My shoulder slammed against a cabinet. The door flew open, revealing a vast wall of shelves that contained vials of deep-red liquid. One of them teetered on a broken rack and fell to the floor, breaking into a million pieces.

"Noooo!" Grigsby screamed.

"Dude, no use crying over spilled Ichor artificial blood,"[15] I said. "There's plenty of that here. Now will you please tell me what's going on?"

"*Ferrous, we don't have time for this!*"

"You brought me to Ichor, Grigsby. You have only a few minutes to explain what all those dead people and animals are doing in that room—and what the heck *this* room is for! And if you don't, I am going to report everything the way *I* see it."

Grigsby sighed. She looked like she was about to cry. "Okay. Okay. First things first . . ."

She began tapping on a laptop keyboard, staring at some instructions on the monitor. Before my eyes, I began to shed clothes.[16] And then I began to shed skin, until I was a skeleton fretted with veins, arteries, muscles, and tendons, like something in a museum of natural history. I was frozen in my tracks, fixed on the sight as everything began to magnify, as if I were plunging headfirst into my own bloodstream. . . .

---

15 Comes in twenty-eight flavors, including Ay-Yi Iron-Rich, Yummy Anemia, Clots-a-Lot, and Extra Salty.

16 Meaning my hologram!

Until I was staring at a really ugly, twisted ladder of globby stuff.

Grigsby smiled wanly. "Say hello to your DNA."

"My . . . *what*?"

Grigs turned her monitor toward me. It showed two long horizontal strings of letters, one string across the top and another across the bottom. The letters were lined up in pairs.

"Watch this." She clicked the mouse, and suddenly a whole bunch of the letters changed colors—and then changed to different letters. She kept clicking the mouse so that the letters toggled back and forth between the original ones and the new ones.

"That's . . . *me*? Why?"

"They have been watching you all your life, Ferrous. They have mapped your genome."

"Because I'm a mutant. . . ."

"The point is, I think they've figured out what to do about it."

I felt my heart jump, like a twanged rubber band. "They found a . . . a . . ." I couldn't bring myself to say the word.

"A cure?" Grigsby said. She was smiling, her eyes brimming with tears. "I don't know for sure, since I'm not supposed to know anything . . . but that's what it looks like."

I couldn't believe my ears. "I—I'm going to be one of you? Dead and immortal? Really?"

I sat at the laptop and watched the DNA letters. I couldn't believe my good fortune. I wanted to sing. I wanted to lift Grigsby off her chair and dance around the room.

But I couldn't move. Questions were zinging around in my brain, slowly coming together. Somehow, it didn't all make sense.

"Grigs . . . why haven't they told me? Why haven't *you*?"

"I've been afraid to tell you. If anyone found out that I'd discovered this place, they would discorporate me." Grigsby was looking at her watch now. "Look, Ferrous, we have only ten minutes, and I'm in big trouble. Those bodies . . . that gross stuff—"

"Are they connected to this?" I asked.

"Of course not! That's the thing, Ferrous. Ichor is a good company. They do good things. Artificial blood, genetic stuff to help you. *So what's up with that room?*"

"I thought you knew," I said.

"No! All I know is that I'm in trouble, and I may take the blame for something very bad that's happening here!"

"How am I supposed to know anything?" I asked.

"You're smart. You know how to think. You're my friend. I can trust you." Grigsby leaned closer. "*Ferrous, those cadavers—they're not complete!*"

My stomach blipped. "Like, you mean, missing body parts?"

"I mean, missing *people*. Not all the bins are accounted for. There are more bins than there are bodies."

"What happened to them?"

Grigsby grabbed my arm. "Ferrous, Sundance is not among them. Her body is not in the morgue. I looked everywhere. They saw me talking to her. They think I hid her, or killed her. If she's not found . . ."

I began pacing. "Okay, in one room, they're trying to cure me. In the other room, they're killing humans. Interesting. Both of those things *create* vampires—"

"Revenants."

95

"Whatever. Okay, don't you think that's weird? Why create them? I mean, it's been drummed in our heads in school—the Undead stay Undead. If you bite humans, you create new Undead. The population grows until you reach Hooper's Limit,[17] and we all start destroying each other. So we should be working to control population, not increase it." I thought a moment, staring at the screen, where the genetic code was blinking on and off. "That gene thing they discovered in me . . . do you think it's like a toggle—one way human, the other revenant? Maybe they're actually working to go the other way. Not to turn humans into revs, but to turn revenants into . . ."

"Ferrous, that is sick!" Grigsby said.

"And what about those mutant killer animals that create other mutant killer animals with one bite? Is that just some kind of jolly company experiment?"

Grigsby suddenly glanced at her watch. Her white skin became almost transparent with fright. "Ferrous, it's six minutes to sunrise."

Yikes.

We bolted up from our chairs and ran for the door. But someone began to push it open from the hallway.

Grigsby pulled me back.

An Ichor worker? Here? *Now?* This could not be happening. We could not be discovered!

We slid behind a bank of wires and machinery. I could hear a

---

17 Also known as Hooper's MUSP, or Maximum Undead Saturation Point (6.23174×10^9), the theoretical absolute maximum number of revenants tolerable on the Earth at any given time. After Joachim Hooper, theoretical macroeconomist, d. 1917, discorporated by a rival revenant scientist 1976.

swishing sound. Footfalls gliding quietly across the floor. A clinking of glass.

Grigsby's eyes radiated confusion and panic. I tried to send her a mental message of comfort. Ichor employees were revs, too. This close to sunrise, they would need to leave pronto. They *couldn't* stick around long. We would wait them out and then make a break.

But Grigsby was about to explode. A small squeal escaped her lips and before I could react, she was on her feet, screaming.

I bolted upward, too. A tall figure, shrouded in black, was racing out into the hallway.

Grigsby leaped toward the door, but she slipped on the broken vial of blood and tumbled to the floor. As I lifted her to her feet, I noticed a rack of vials had been taken from the cabinet and put on the console. One of the vials was missing. "That was . . . a *thief*," I said.

"*Come on—now!*" Grigsby was out the door. She couldn't have cared less about the intruder. This was a matter of death.

I followed close behind. I could see the black form ahead of us. He was fast. He seemed to be practically flowing along the curved corridor.

We reached the transub station in seconds. This time, I barely noticed the pain as we melded through the granite.

The New York City night appeared before us, the distant lights from the West Side flickering through the trees. The air rushed into my lungs, and I had to gasp for breath.

"Ohhhhh . . ." Grigsby sounded awful. I looked at her and knew she was in trouble. Her body was pulsating. Her fingertips already looked translucent.

It was still dark, but I didn't dare look behind me, toward the east. "Two minutes . . . fifteen . . . sec . . ." Grigsby was gasping.

"Stop talking and move!" I shouted, pulling her into the park.

The stranger was ahead of us, faltering, leaning against the Parks Department shed. The sound of our footsteps caused the figure to leap ahead, trying to rise above the ground, making distance in ever-weakening leaps.

The Belvedere spire came into view, and I tried to pick up speed. "Hold . . . me . . ." Grigsby rasped.

I lifted her onto my back. For the first time in my life, I was glad to be a Blooder. I could do this. I could outlast the sunrise.

She weighed so little, I could carry her at a run. In moments, I could see the base of the Crypt in the Rock. It was deserted, all the revenants safely inside, in a peaceful death-sleep.

"One minute, three . . . seconds . . ." Grigsby whispered into my ear. Her hand felt like film. She was entering the first stages of discorporation, where the body starts going into what our teacher, Mr. McAbre, used to call the Dance of Death.

"Hang on, we're almost there!" I shouted.

I raced past an old oak tree. And my foot caught.

I felt myself flying forward. Off balance. I heard a shrieking cry and realized it was my own voice. Grigsby was flying off my shoulder.

I hit the ground hard, my body twisted so that I could see what I had tripped over.

Or *whom*.

The hooded figure lay sprawled by the tree, writhing in agony from where my foot had made contact.

"He . . . help . . . Fe . . . Ferrous . . ."

The dark hood turned, revealing a familiar face.

The thief was Max.

"What were *you* doing . . ." I began. There were a million things I wanted to ask him, but I plugged it. I sprang to my feet. I could sense that the air was changing. It felt charged, energized by some kind of predawn near-light.

"Right . . . pocket . . ." he said, pointing to his pants.

I reached inside and pulled out a vial of red liquid.

"Why?" I asked. "Why did you steal this, Max? *What is it?*"

He was opening his mouth, indicating I was to feed him. He was desperate.

I glanced at Grigsby, who was getting fainter by the moment. But if this could help Max, maybe it could help her, too. So I poured the stuff down his throat and hoped he knew what he was doing.

He choked and coughed but seemed to get it down. "I'll be . . . fine now."

"Should I give some to Grigs?" I said. "Do you have more?"

"I only . . . took . . . one vial. . . ."

No.

I scooped up Grigsby, who was shedding a paper-thin layer of skin.

Like an onion, Mr. McAbre used to say. *It starts in layers. . . .*

I realized I could see her now. Not in the amber streetlamp glow but in the first silver-gray haze of the morning light.

As I brought her to the base of the rock, I heard a soft *tssss . . . tssss . . .* and realized it was the sound of my tears dripping on her skin and vaporizing.

"Touch her to the rock," Max said, his voice stronger. "The

smooth part, just below the electrical station."

I dragged her to the smooth spot and mumbled the incantation she always used—but nothing happened. *"You do it!"* I shouted to Max. *"You're the vampire!"*

Max's eyes were different—confused, desperate, and lightless. But also, somehow, joyful. "No, actually, I'm not," he said.

"This is no time to correct my grammar!" I said.

"I'm not a rev. Or a vampire. Not anymore." He was feeling himself now, as if he'd just switched bodies. "I'm cured, Ferrous. . . ."

"Salada . . . dichtu . . . ," Grigsby was murmuring. *"Moriere . . . datu . . ."*

Her head rolled to the side.

"Nooo!" I screamed. *"Nimachtano!* Say it! Say it! *Help me, Max."*

I felt Max's hand touching my shoulder. "Let her mort," he said.

"What?"

"It's the right thing, Ferrous. It's what we all need to do. To sacrifice. For the good of the whole."

I stared at him in shock. And that was when I saw it for the first time—his black shirt was ripped to the waist, and I could see a tattoo of intertwining snakes.

The twin letters *I* of Ichor Institute.

"I don't believe this . . . ," I murmured. "You're one of them."

Max was grinning. "It works. The derevenation serum *works*, Ferrous. I'm like you now. I will die someday. Really die. They promised they were working on it. They said they were using your genome. I didn't think they could do it. All those sacrifices. All those humans I had to round up for them. Some of them were so awful."

"Sundance . . ." I murmured. It was all becoming clear.

Max rolled his eyes. "She was the worst! They were going to try one batch on her. It was between that batch and another. Genes are tricky. The slightest variation . . . Anyway, they weren't sure which would work. Certain versions of the serum, I'm told, would transform subjects into hideous beasts. Predators who have the power to make other predators. They said to come back in a few days, when they found the correct formula. They said they'd show me the genetics lab, give me a sample. But I couldn't wait. When I saw you and Grigsby in the woods, I had a feeling you'd be going there. . . ."

Now that he was human, I wanted to kill him.

But I had a more important task. I ignored him, whispering into Grigsby's ear: "*Nimachtano! Nimachtano!* Come on, say it, Grigs!"

"I will feel what it's like to fall in love," Max went on, "to catch a cold, to taste ice cream. Look at me. I'm real! *I'm real!*"

I could feel Grigsby tightening her grip on my hand. As feathery as she was, she was trying to comfort me. She knew what was on my mind—they had used me. They had used *my* genetic code. They had figured out how to work the DNA. To turn things on and off.

Human . . . revenant . . . human . . . revenant . . .

"It's a new world," Max said. "You're the lucky one, Ferrous. More and more of us will volunteer to become like you. Mortal. By our sacrifice we will trim the population, for the greater enjoyment of all revenants."

"Stop it!" I screamed, glaring at him. "I know you, Max. You're a fake. You're going to wait this out. You're going to make sure other revenants discorporate—like Grigsby. And then, one day, you're going to use the serum to toggle back."

Max's resolute look faltered. "Are you accusing me . . . ?"

Grigsby turned. She looked directly at Max. "*Ni . . . mach . . . tano!*"

Suddenly the dust began to swirl around her. The smooth section of rock became like a sludge, roiling and bubbling and dark.

There was a sound like a muted kettledrum, and she was gone—hidden now, safely in the crypt.

"Well," Max said. "That was dramatic." He brushed himself off and breathed deeply, his skin a ruddy shade I had never seen before. "This will be it, I guess. I'm off to the real world."

I was exhausted and sad. "Good riddance," I said.

He put a warm hand on my shoulder. "Why don't you come with me? We'll get an apartment. Start a business."

"*What?*"

"Transformations! Ladies and gents, feel what it's like to be a vampire! Or a hideous, carnivorous beast. Bite your friends. For a bigger fee, kill your enemies!"

The sun was brightening now. I squinted up at him, my eyes stinging. He didn't seem to be affected by the brightness much. Already we were different.

But we had always been different. It didn't matter what form we took. I knew, in that moment, I would be happy to stay just the way I was. "You are a total jerk," I said.

Max shrugged. "Suit yourself. See you in the graveyard!"

He turned to go, his face angled toward the sun. Part of me wanted to run after him, to convince him to change his mind, to make him give me the serum and let me become what I had always wanted to be.

Instead, I turned back to the rock as Max's footsteps clopped against the walkway.

He wasn't flitting anymore.

AAAAWWWWWWK!

From across the meadow, an animal sound ripped the morning sky. I turned and saw the violent flap of giant wings. Sharp talon points descending.

Instinctively I ducked. But the hawk was nowhere near me.

It swooped right for Max's red, fleshy neck, planting its claws deeply.

He screamed, trying to rip the animal free. But he wasn't as strong as he used to be, and that huge bird was not to be moved.

The two of them fell forward into the shadows of a hedge. I leaped to my feet. I didn't want the hawk to target me next, but I was curious. I picked up a large branch for defense, just in case.

As I edged closer to the hedge, the sun's rays were suffusing the park with dim light. I caught a glimpse of the MISSING HEIRESS sign on the sycamore tree.

I stared at it. I thought about the bin. The tiara.

And I dropped the stick. Because in that moment, I knew.

When I looked back into the shadow, I saw the hawk rise up into the sky.

In its talons was an enormous, struggling rat.

ABOUT THE AUTHORS

Neal Shusterman

Neal Shusterman is the award-winning author of more than thirty books for young adults. His books include *Unwind*, *The Schwa Was Here*, *Full Tilt*, *Downsiders*, *The Shadow Club*, and many more.

Often funny, sometimes dark, but always thought-provoking, Neal's books stretch the limits of imagination and defy the traditional concept of genre. In fact, Neal considers himself a "genre buster."

As a film and television writer, Neal worked on the *Goosebumps* and *Animorphs* TV series and wrote the Disney Channel film *Pixel Perfect*. Currently he is adapting his novel *Everlost* as a feature film for Universal Studios.

"Perpetual Pest" marks his first official collaboration with Terry Black. "Both Terry and I have bizarre imaginations and absurd senses of humor," Neal says, "so we knew if we put our heads together, we would . . . uh . . . *dig up* something great."

Neal lives in Southern California with his four children, who are a constant source of inspiration.

Terry Black

Terry Black writes books, movies, TV shows, cartoons, computer games, short stories, and comic books. His work for *Tales from the Crypt* on HBO won him a CableACE Award. Currently he's writing the interactive games Red Steel 2 and I Am Alive for Unisoft. Terry also wrote the film *Dead Heat*, a cop zombie horror/comedy starring Treat Williams and Joe Piscopo, now available on DVD. He's written for the TV series *Dark Justice, Silk Stalkings, 18 Wheels of Justice*, and *Tales from the Cryptkeeper*. He also writes for *Alfred Hitchcock Mystery Magazine, Leading Edge Magazine of Science Fiction and Fantasy, Tales of the Unanticipated*, and the underground comic book *Pete the P.O.'d Postal Worker*, published by Sharkbait Press.

Terry lives in Mission Viejo, California, with a black cat named Satchmo, who brings home live rabbits and an occasional slice of ham.

Ellen Wittlinger

Ellen Wittlinger is the author of fourteen novels for young adults, including such titles as *Sandpiper*; *Blind Faith*; *Parrotfish*; *Love & Lies*; and her forthcoming book, *This Means War!* Her novel *Hard Love* won a Michael L. Printz Honor Award and a Lambda Literary Award. Many of her novels have been listed on the annual "best books" lists of the New York Public Library and the American Library Association; she has also won state book awards in Massachusetts, Michigan, and Pennsylvania. Wittlinger's novels have been translated into French, German, Dutch, Danish, Turkish, Italian, Croatian, and Korean. A former children's librarian, she lives with her husband in western Massachusetts.

About the writing of "Ghost Dog," she says, "Since I got my rescue dog, Woody, last year, I've been thinking about dogs all the time, so it's no surprise that one made its way into this story, too. Doesn't everybody love to read about dogs?"

For more information about Ellen, visit her Web site at www.ellenwittlinger.com.

Christopher Paul Curtis

Christopher Paul Curtis was born in Flint, Michigan, where, as many Flintstones did, he went to work right after high school in one of the city's automobile factories. His job was to put the driver's door on big Buicks. He did this for thirteen years. To this day, he shudders every time he gets into or out of any large vehicle. Especially Buicks.

He is the author of *The Watsons Go to Birmingham—1963* (Newbery Honor, Coretta Scott King Honor); *Bud, Not Buddy* (Newbery Medal, Coretta Scott King Award); *Bucking the Sarge*; *Mr. Chickee's Funny Money*; *Mr. Chickee's Messy Mission*; and *Elijah of Buxton* (Newbery Honor, Coretta Scott King Award).

He says, "Writing 'Going Old School in the Age of Obama' was especially rewarding since I was able to shine a light on a group of people who have been the victims of years and years of bad press and outright lies. I'm always happy to set the record straight."

Douglas Rees

Douglas Rees says:

"I was born in a military hospital at March Air Force Base in Southern California. This was rather a long time ago now.

"After a pretty typical upbringing, with several moves around the country and the world, I ended up back where I'd started—to finish high school, go to school, and get married.

"I was always dodging the fact that what I wanted to do was write. Finally I realized that no one else was ever going to write my books if I didn't, and started working systematically. Since then, I've had six novels published—and now, my first short story.

"'Anasazi Breakdown' had its origin in a trip my wife and I took to Chaco Canyon, New Mexico. While I didn't find the place eerie or frightening, the ancientness of the place, in a country that thinks of its history as beginning in 1492, was strange in itself. Something like that feeling underlies this story."

Kevin Emerson

Kevin Emerson is a former elementary school science teacher. He currently teaches writing at 826 Seattle, and with Seattle Writers in the Schools.

Kevin has been writing stories since he was a kid growing up in Cheshire, Connecticut. He wrote his first "novel" in sixth grade, about a fearless secret agent.

When he is not writing, camping with his wife, Annie, and daughter, Willow, or tending to the tomato plants, Kevin is busy as a musician. His band, Central Services, in which he sings and plays drums, has charted nationally on college radio. The band just finished a kids' record called *The Board of Education*.

"The Coffin Deliveries" is based on an idea Kevin had while walking around the Dorchester, Massachusetts, neighborhood where he used to teach. He also loves getting packages by mail, and is always curious what his neighbors are getting, too.

Learn more about Kevin at www.kevinemerson.net. Dive into his Oliver Nocturne series at www.olivernocturne.com. Hear hilarious songs about tomatoes, commas, tinfoil, and more at www.thelonelytomato.com.

Joshua Gee

Joshua Gee first learned about the dangerous lives of werewolves while writing the award-winning *Encyclopedia Horrifica: The Terrifying TRUTH! About Vampires, Ghosts, Monsters, and More.* According to eyewitnesses, he is frequently sighted in New York City and at www.joshuagee.com.

Peter Lerangis

Peter Lerangis, while jogging through Central Park one morning, spotted a red-tailed hawk savagely attacking an empty plastic water bottle, stumbling each time it tried to fly away, as the prey slipped from its talons. He began wondering what on earth that bird was thinking. And from that image, this story grew.

Peter is the award-winning author of more than 160 books, including two titles in The 39 Clues series; the entire Spy X, Abracadabra, and Watchers series; as well as the Antarctica duo and the historical novel *Smiler's Bones*. He has traveled to Russia on Air Force One with former First Lady Laura Bush and speaks extensively at schools all over the world. Among his many death-defying life exploits are earning a degree in biochemical sciences from Harvard, running a marathon, acting professionally in the musical theater, rock climbing in Yosemite National Park during a 6.1 earthquake, and singing a cappella.

He and his wife, the musician Tina deVaron, live in New York City with their two college-student sons, Nick and Joe.

Lois Metzger, Editor

Lois Metzger is the author of several young-adult novels, including *Missing Girls* (a *New York Times* Best Book for Children), and many short stories for anthologies all over the world.

In addition to editing *Bites* and its companion volume, *Bones: Terrifying Tales to Haunt Your Dreams*, she has edited three other collections for Scholastic: *The Year We Missed My Birthday, Can You Keep a Secret?*, and *Be Careful What You Wish For*. She has also written two nonfiction books—*Yours, Anne: The Life of Anne Frank* and *The Hidden Girl: A True Story of the Holocaust* (with Lola Rein Kaufman).

She lives in New York City with her husband and son.

ACKNOWLEDGMENTS

Special thanks to Gabrielle Balkan, Linda Ferreira, Elizabeth Krych, Janet Kusmierski, Arthur A. Levine, Judy Newman, Andrea Davis Pinkney, and Roy Wandelmaier at Scholastic, and to Susan Cohen and Ellen Datlow . . .

. . . and to all the writers who contributed to this book, for their hard work, excellent stories, and unsurpassed ability to capture that unexplained, unsettling feeling that comes over you as you realize that something has gone terribly wrong. . . .